The Wicked Wager

BY

ANYA WYLDE

Copyright © 2012 Anya Wylde

All rights reserved.

ISBN:1517724317
ISBN-13:9781517724313

DEDICATION

For John

CONTENTS

ACKNOWLEDGMENTS i

Prologue 2

Chapter 1 7

Chapter 2 14

Chapter 3 19

Chapter 4 25

Chapter 5 30

Chapter 6 39

Chapter 7 45

Chapter 8 50

Chapter 9 56

Chapter 10 61

Chapter 11 67

Chapter 12 72

Chapter 13 78

Chapter 14 84

Chapter 15 90

Chapter 16 98

Chapter 17 106

Chapter 18 111

Chapter 19 115

Chapter 20	121
Chapter 21	127
Chapter 22	133
Chapter 23	140
Chapter 24	147
Chapter 25	154
Chapter 26	163
Chapter 27	170
Chapter 28	179
Chapter 29	186
Chapter 30	193
Epilogue	201
ABOUT THE AUTHOR	204
Other Books By The Author	205

ACKNOWLEDGMENTS

Thank you, Ashish, for reading my first novel (currently buried in my back yard) and encouraging me to write in spite of it.
Thank you, John, for your unconditional love and support, but mostly I thank you for the endless cups of tea.
Thank you, Kirsten, for all your help.

Prologue

The Honourable Earl of Hamilton flung his brown, exquisitely tailored buckskin breeches over one shoulder and leaped out of the window.

He landed on a prickly bush.

Curtailing an urge to squeal as the sharp thorns dug into his flesh. He scrambled up.

"He jumped, ma!" A whiny feminine voice floated down from the first-floor window.

After a quick worried glance upwards, the Earl somersaulted over the grass and with practised ease slipped behind a looming tree.

"Blast it! He has escaped," a more mature voice growled, poking a grey head out of the window.

The Earl smiled grimly. Yet another unmarried lady had set her cap on him. She had used an age-old trick of trying to seduce him and then having her mother discover them in a compromising position.

He pulled on his breeches and started walking. No simpering, frothy chit could trap him, he thought, puffing out his chest like a proud, multicoloured peacock. He was, after all, an old hand at escaping sticky situations. He had decamped, not only with his bachelorhood intact, but also managed to save his pants and his dignity.

He chuckled softly. His valet would be pleased and his coachman relieved. They were getting tired of finding him lurking around on street corners wearing only his unmentionables or, at times, nothing at all.

"Bloody blooming roses sprouting out of a fairy's arse!"

The Earl skidded to a halt, the smile dying on his lips. Who could possess the voice of an angel and curse like a bloodthirsty pirate? He was intrigued.

He raised his foot to bound ahead and discover the delightful creature when the sensible part of him forced him to pause and think . . . *Was this another ploy of some young miss out to ensnare a husband?*

A skirt rustled somewhere close by.

He tilted his head and his naughty ears trembled impatiently.

Something or someone squeaked softly.

He took a small step forward, and immediately the sensible part of him reared up once more in warning. He had but a moment ago escaped a terrifying virgin — could he afford to test his luck once again? What if this time he was caught and god forbid . . . forced into marrying a giggling, dim-witted creature.

He shuddered. He had noticed an increasing amount of mothers with their unmarried daughters circling around him in ballrooms. He had learned to spot them a mile away. They were beautiful, innocent looking creatures filled with evil complicated plans that involved trapping poor, harmless attractive men like himself into marriage.

Mothers and their daughters, he thought grimly, should be allowed to hunt with rifles. Any young woman actively searching for a mate would bring down more prey than the best of shots in London.

The moon brightened at that moment illuminating a bit of dark green skirt peeking out from behind the tree.

The wise, sensible part of him went quiet.

It was not every day that one heard a cultured voice utter such words aloud. If it was another contrived ploy, then it was a creative one.

He took another cautious step forward. He wondered how a woman from a respectable background learned such an inspired cuss. That she was cultured, he did not doubt. The dignified hiss and the fact that this was the viscount's ball, with only the select upper class invited, ensured the presence of only the well-bred variety.

It could be someone's chaperone, he mused, as he tiptoed towards the tree. The voice, though, had sounded too young to belong to a chaperone, and he truly doubted if a lady in hopes of finding a husband would resort to uttering expletives in dark corners of gardens.

If anything, it would have sent a man with any sense running in the opposite direction.

"Bollocks!" the hidden stranger muttered.

This charming new exclamation decided him, and he quickened

his step. He convinced himself that he was safe from the dangers of matchmaking as his curiosity mounted.

A twig snapped under his foot, sounding like a whiplash in the silent night. He winced at the sound and found a head peering at him from behind the tree.

"Are you all right, madam?" he asked, sending a swift prayer up to anyone who might deal with matters of luck.

There was a beat of silence before the girl gently lifted her skirts and stepped towards him. He briefly cursed the sliver of moonlight that hid more than it showed. The rustle of cloth had sounded like silk, and now he desperately wanted to see her face.

"Yes, My Lord. I felt a little faint from the heat in the ballroom."

That cuss wouldn't have come out of a fainting belle, he thought smirking.

She still stood near the looming tree, which dispersed whatever little light the moon threw out. Her voice sounded vaguely familiar, but he could not place it.

"That was an inventive little oath. Wherever did you hear it first?" he drawled.

A tiny gasp was followed by an outraged silence.

The Earl wanted to grin in delight. He truly shouldn't have mentioned that, but some devilry in him had prompted him. He had been bored with social games, and since the season was ending, his refined edges were fraying.

"You sounded out of temper," he continued. "How can I be of assistance? It is sometimes easier to talk to strangers."

"You, My Lord, are not a stranger."

"Your frigid tones warm my heart. I wonder what you have heard about me. I assure you, I do not bite. Come, tell me what is wrong?"

Again, a beat of silence followed. He could almost hear the wheels turning in her head, her need to unburden her woes warring with her need to behave like a lady and not gossip.

"Miss Clearwater told me that-that I resembled a pea!" came the mortified reply, followed by a shocked gasp. She had clearly not meant to say it.

Ah! The lady in question had her refined edges fraying as well.

"A P?"

"The tiny, disgusting, green vegetable."

"Surely that's nothing to get worked up about? I have heard

women can be a lot more vicious."

He held out his hand and waggled his fingers impatiently. They needed to get back indoors before they were discovered in this dark, lonely part of the garden. And the last thing he wanted at the moment was to be discovered with someone who resembled a little round vegetable.

Her father would likely jump at the chance and insist his lovely daughter had been compromised. Thereafter, he would be doomed to marry her and produce little round green children. The prospect sounded far from being pleasant.

She ignored the hand and continued bitterly. "Yes, it should not have bothered me, but she said it in front of the only man who has shown any interest in me during the entire season. She, being the beauty of the ton, turned her wiles on him, and all my hopes of being married are now dashed, for his eyes glazed over the moment she smiled at him."

"He sounds like an insipid sort of fellow. He should have stood by you instead of being charmed by that cat." He had spoken absently. He was growing concerned about the fact that he was still chatting with this girl, who by her own admission was so unappealing that only a milk faced sop had paid any attention to her the entire season.

His eyes warily tracked the dark looming shadows, wondering if one of them was her father waiting for the right moment to pop out and declare a quick trip to Gretna Green was now in order.

Her giggle snapped his attention back. She had a pretty laugh.

"You haven't been deceived by her looks, My Lord?"

"Anyone with more wit than the hair on his head can tell that the young Miss Clearwater, however well packaged, is dangerous."

"I suppose there is always next year."

"I am sure you will make an excellent match next season, miss. Now, we truly should be going indoors. You must be getting chilled."

"I am perfectly fine, and the evening is uncommonly hot. You can go, My Lord. I want to stay out here a little longer."

"I cannot leave a young lady unattended. Please take my arm now," he commanded.

The girl ignored him. Instead, she picked up her skirts and ran in the opposite direction of the house.

He groaned and took off after her. He knew she didn't want her identity known. Not after that florid outburst and all she had revealed in her agitation, but he was in no mood to play games.

He could see the outline of her running figure, and her slight build put him in mind of a wood nymph. Her emerald dress sparkled in the light of the various lamps around the garden path. He increased his speed as she turned the corner and momentarily disappeared from his sight.

He paused. He should leave her to her fate. He was a rake, after all. But then his conscience intervened. He may be a rake, but he had always been a gentleman rake.

They had reached the end of the garden before he caught up with her. He was impressed with her pace, giving him his first clue as to who she was—someone who had assuredly spent her life in the country.

He grabbed her hand and brought her to a stop. Before she could even think of struggling in his grip, he forced her to turn around. She was afraid of his discovering her identity, so once he knew it, she would stop this nonsense of trying to escape him.

He stared down into a delicate face now bathed in moonlight. Long gold lashes rimmed eyes the colour of new budding leaves. Her mouth was a full pink, her features fragile. Shock had him rooted to the spot. This was no wallflower, no ugly miss.

This was the extremely beautiful, Emma Grey.

The reason no one had approached her was not due to lack of beauty or birth but because she had three very big, very surly and very possessive elder brothers. Her brothers eyed any man hovering in Emma's vicinity with undisguised menace.

The Earl had been introduced to her and danced with her once, all the while holding her as far away from him as possible lest her brothers were watching. He had wisely left her alone after that.

He should have remembered his wisdom then. He should have recalled her burly brothers to mind. He should have dropped his hands and quickly made his way back.

He didn't. Instead, he foolishly kissed her and then promptly fell in love.

Chapter 1

The ton was aflutter when they discovered the news of Miss Emma Grey snaring the most eligible bachelor of the season.

The society papers were full of the romantic match, and even the most conservative of the lot approved. Miss Grey was, after all, the daughter of a respectable man next in line for a Dukedom.

Emma's father, Lord Grey, was the first cousin of the Duke of Arden and next in line to inherit. The Duke had no other male heirs and was of considerable age; hence, the title was sure to pass on to Lord Grey.

All that Lord Grey had to do was wait and pray for his dear cousin to depart for heaven and sooner done the better.

Lady Grey was delighted to be sure. Emma was nineteen, having missed the first two seasons of coming out. The first season Emma's grandfather had died, and the next year was followed by the death of her grandmother. Her darling daughter, in the year of her debut, had snatched the young, handsome and superbly wealthy Richard Hamilton from under the very nose of Miss Clearwater. Nothing could have made her happier.

Meanwhile, Emma had spent the entire season wondering if she were a homely sort. She refused to believe the compliments of her loved ones. She didn't think she would ever find a man, since most men under the age of fifty, married or otherwise, barely looked her in the eye and departed as soon as common courtesy allowed.

She soon learned the reason when Lord Hamilton hesitatingly requested her to speak to her brothers and beg them to spare his life.

Understandably furious, Emma took her three brothers to task. The five feet four inches tall girl faced her six foot muscled brothers and gave them a tongue lashing that they never forgot.

In spite of the terror their sister had induced in them, they still refused to allow the Earl to court her.

Lord Hamilton proved his love and devotion for Emma in the only way a man can prove his worth. Nights out in pubs with contests as to who could drink more ale followed for the next few weeks. After that came archery competitions and horse racing.

Lord Hamilton proved his might and successfully and cleverly won over the three surly brothers.

A month later, looking pale and worn out, he finally presented his proposal to Emma's father and was accepted.

You would think the trials for the lovers were now over. The brothers were agreeable, the parents pleased, and the ton approved.

Yet, the biggest hurdle was still to be faced. The Duke of Arden heard of the engagement, and thus began the most difficult battle the two had ever faced.

❖ ❖ ❖

Emma nibbled her bottom lip worriedly. "Richard, we have a problem."

"What is it?" the Earl asked absently.

They were taking a carriage ride around town, and having his betrothed so close to him was proving to be awfully tempting. He wanted to grab her and kiss her. The occasional brush of her skirt and her being completely unaware of his state was frustrating to say the least.

The last thing he wanted was to have an extended engagement. He was the kind of man, who once made up his mind, stuck to his resolution and tried to finish off the task as speedily as possible.

The fact that his fiancée was so very desirable had him wishing that they didn't have to wait a full two months before the wedding occurred.

His protests had been shot down, not only by his future mother-in-law, but also by his future bride. Neither of them could fathom how a wedding could be organised in anything less than three months. Two months was all the compromise they were willing to offer.

Emma turned towards him. "Do you know my uncle, the Duke of Arden?"

"No. He retired to the country before I graced society, and prior to that I was at Oxford."

"Well, yes, but you know of him?" she asked impatiently.

"Who does not?" he asked grumpily.

"His daughter, Catherine and I spend our summers together. We are very close, and the Duke is exceedingly fond of me, and he . . . he heard of the engagement."

The Earl heard the slight tremor in her voice. He turned to look at her and noticed for the first time that something was troubling her.

He would have noticed earlier, but his mind had been preoccupied with trying to keep his hands off her. He wanted to be respectable and start his marriage on the right footing. His *Cherie Amie* had been politely told to retire and compensated well for her expertise. Now he wanted to be a perfect gentleman, honourable to his vows and faithful to his wife.

He could not afford to ruin his new found resolutions by tumbling in the hay with his fiancée.

"Is the Duke against the marriage?" he asked, feeling slightly ill.

"No, no . . . it's not that. His Grace is pleased, or rather delighted that I am engaged. He has even invited us to have our wedding in a church near his home. You would admire him greatly. He has been so generous to our family. My father often seeks his advice on important matters — "

"You are babbling, my dear. Now, out with it."

She took a deep breath and let the words out in a rush. "He wants us to wait a year."

"No!" he exploded.

This would not do, not do at all. He would never be able to stay celibate for an entire year. He was, after all, a hot-blooded man.

The Duke had no right to dictate to him about how and when his wedding occurred. He would not allow it. Two months had seemed like an eternity, and the thought of delaying the wedding for a year had him breaking out in a cold sweat.

"For one moment stop thinking about the marriage bed and hear me out," Emma snapped.

The Earl turned to stare at his fiancée. He should be used to her shocking ways by now . . . but he was not. She continuously surprised him with her boldness. In fact, she had made three dames swoon at the last ball they had attended together.

He shook his head disapprovingly. If anyone had the right to scandalize the ton, then it was him. But now that they were getting married, he had tamed his behaviour somewhat. However, his future bride was another matter.

He would have to take her in hand, starting now.

"Why do you think I was thinking of the marriage bed? Are you?" he asked silkily.

She blushed.

That calmed the Earl down. At least she had a modicum of maidenly modesty intact.

"No . . . that is what my mother told me. She told me to be careful around you because men had only one thing on their mind."

The Earl scowled, regardless of the fact that her mother had told her exactly what he had been struggling with a few moments ago.

"I can control myself," he bit out.

"So, then you will have no trouble waiting a year," she responded slyly.

He smiled in appreciation of her tactic. But he was far cleverer than she gave him credit for, and he was not willing to wait any longer.

"I will not wait longer than two months," he said firmly. "I desire you too much." If she could not curb her wild tongue, then nor would he.

Emma was stunned into silence. She had hoped to rile him up and have him defend his position as a gentleman. She had not expected him to admit he wanted her too much to wait.

She felt curiously thrilled at the thought. His kisses had told her enough to know that the result would not be entirely unpleasant.

She took a trembling breath. "Still . . . we cannot marry for a year. My father cannot afford to alienate the Duke since he is next in line to inherit. The Duke might decide to take another heir if we displease him. We have to heed his wishes. Can you imagine our third cousin, Mr Barwinkle, becoming the next Duke?" she pleaded. "Why, he looks like a flea bitten rabbit!"

The Earl was silent.

"Please don't be angry, Richard. My family cannot disregard his request on such an important matter. He is really quite reasonable. I am sure once I plead my case, he will reconsider," she placed a soothing hand on his shoulder. "I am planning to visit him and convince him. He must have a good reason for asking us to delay the wedding. I simply need to prove to him that I have made the right choice. I will allay his concerns, and he is intelligent enough to listen to reason."

The Earl grew more and more annoyed all through Emma's speech. Their courtship had been quick, and he had not yet spent enough time with her to know her well. Her brothers had kept him busy during most of their relationship. A few moments alone together with an abigail keeping a close eye on them was hardly enough time to learn her character.

She had agreed to marry him and seemed to like him, but neither of them had mentioned love. Love was unfashionable, and marriages were made according to status.

The Earl, however, when it came to taking a wife, held very old fashioned views. He loved her . . . but he did not know her. It was a confounding experience.

He scratched his head and cocked his head towards her.

She was still speaking. Her voice full of warmth, her face alight and a soft dreamy smile playing on her lips.

He shifted uneasily. This was the first time he had fallen in love, and it left him feeling insecure and uncertain. He felt for a moment like that blasted Shakespearean character . . . What was his name? Ah, yes . . . Iago. Consumed with irrational jealousy.

He narrowed his eyes. How could someone as beautiful, refined and graceful as her, love a man like him? What if she did not love him but the Duke? Sure, the Duke was possibly bald, missing teeth, potbellied, her relative and what not, but the way she was waxing lyrical about him made it entirely possible.

He straightened in his seat and said condescendingly, "You have not been in the world long enough to judge a man, my dear. He must be full of faults that you have overlooked."

"I am not witless. I know an intelligent man from a buffoon. The Duke is the best of men," she snapped, thoroughly angry at his sneering tone.

She turned her face away from him.

"Look at me," he demanded. "I do not fancy having a conversation with your fish shaped bun pin."

She crossed her eyes and stuck her tongue out at him. "If you think I will be one of those dull flower pot wives with no opinions of her own, then you are wrong. I shall not fade into the background and listen and agree to every foolish whim of yours. I have a mind of my own and intend to keep it. I shall not leave it behind in my mother's house after the wedding."

Her tirade halted when the carriage lurched into a pot hole, and she was thrown against him.

He, for once, did not notice or care. His fiancée should have been moony-eyed and not found him wanting in any way. He was raging with jealousy and could not wait to get rid of her.

He glared out of the window. They were nearly at her townhouse. He kept his eyes resolutely on the blackened London streets, choosing to watch soot faced urchins rather than the beautiful woman next to him.

His resolution broke soon enough and he peeked at her from the corner of his eyes. He found her turning puce in rage. Her fingers were digging into his beautiful soft leather seats. Her nails would probably leave permanent indentations.

He tossed his head and sniffed loudly. He would rather she tear the expensive leather and mangle the carriage than have her bad tempered fingers attach themselves to his arm.

He rapped the carriage walls in a signal to his coachman to speed up the horses.

It was in mutual relief that the two parted that evening.

❖ ❖ ❖

The Earl was in his cups. He told his valet the whole sordid story.

The valet, in turn, had a hard time keeping his face straight.

"I am a man, am I not? That old bugger would not turn a hair, even if a naked wench danced on his lap. That is if he has any hair. While Emma . . . " The Earl stopped to take a big gulp of brandy. "Emma is beautiful and desirable, but her tongue comes out with the wickedest things. It is positively entertaining when directed at others, but I am her fiancé, for goodness' sake. Do you know Burns? That Duke . . . that old blighter has made my lovely Emma fall in love with him. I wish I could do something . . . anything! What do you suggest, Burns?"

The valet coughed and bent to refill the Earl's glass. His portly belly jiggled as he said, "She is marrying you, My Lord, and not the Duke. I would say that she loves you, but maybe for your peace of mind you should ensure that she recognises your intelligence as being more finely honed than the Duke's. After all, one's wife should never doubt your capabilities. You will have trouble controlling her fanciful ways if she goes running to the Duke for every tiny piece of advice. I mean, imagine," continued the valet, warming to his topic, "that she wanted to buy six pieces of fish, and you tell her to buy seven in case something happens to one of the pieces of fish. Mayhap it gets overcooked or burns? But she . . . does she listen to you? No, sir, she does not! Instead, she goes to your elder brother, and he tells her to buy eight. Eight mind you, not seven, in case two of the fish get burnt or overcooked. So here you are thinking of economy and the fact that you have to spend on a dinner of six. Instead, you end up paying for eight. Now, tell me, where is the wisdom in that? It's perfectly disgraceful to have your wife listen to your elder brother and not you," finished the valet, trembling with emotion.

"Here, have a brandy."

"Thank you, sir, I think I will."

The two sipped in silence for a while until a huge smile lit the Earl's face.

"Burns, old chap, you are brilliant! That's it. I know exactly what to do. If you were a maid, I would have kissed you."

"Thank you, sir, but please recall I am a man and not a maid," replied the stoic valet.

"And, Burns, next time your wife buys an extra fish, allow me to pay for it."

"Very good, sir."

Chapter 2

Emma paced the length of the morning room.

Her mother hid a smile. "This is just a lover's quarrel. You will have many such in the coming months. Don't scowl, my dear. It makes you look ghastly."

Emma scowled harder. The Earl had captured her heart the first time he had spoken to her. And like every other female during the season, she, too, had appreciated his good looks.

His face was chiselled bones and angles, and his blonde hair looked temptingly soft. His best features were his cornflower blue eyes that sparkled with mischief at all times.

He had been a rake, leaving more hearts broken than any other man during the season. He enjoyed speaking his mind, particularly unsettling those of the starched variety. His very nature had appealed to her, which was so like her own.

Yet, all through that first dance, he had treated her as if she were infested with fleas. His coldness had hurt more than anyone else's indifference.

When he had proposed, she had been the happiest girl in England.

She stopped pacing and abruptly sat down. She tried composing her face into an expressionless mask. Multiple deep breaths later, she gave up. It was impossible. She couldn't help but worry.

She reflected on his faults — his arrogance and his possessiveness. She could handle the possessiveness. After living with her three elder brothers, the Earl was relatively tame. The arrogance was what bothered her. She was a thinking being. She could not blindly believe that her fiancé had no faults. No man was perfect, and it was unfair of Richard to expect her to believe otherwise.

Admittedly, she had gone on about the Duke deliberately to annoy him. Some imp inside her had pushed her to do so. Perhaps it was the frustration of waiting and the fear of something going wrong to stop the wedding.

There was yet another thing which Emma had kept from the Earl. She would be leaving for the Duke's residence in a week, and her return was indefinite.

It could be months before they saw each other again. At a time when their courtship was still so new, to give the relationship a break was troubling her. What if he fell in love with someone else? They still had so much to learn about each other, and every moment together was precious. With an unhappy sigh, she picked up the sewing.

A glance at the clock showed he was late for his usual morning call. She worriedly stabbed the cloth, wondering if she had gone too far by arguing with him the last time they had met.

She had just finished stitching a leaf when the butler announced the Earl's arrival.

Emma forced herself to stay seated when all she wanted to do was leap up and run to the door.

The Earl entered the room and jovially greeted them.

Emma searched his face and apart from a few tired lines around his mouth, found him in an amiable mood.

She could tell he was eager to speak to her alone, and sure enough he asked her mother's permission to allow them to take a stroll in the park.

Emma leaped up and headed towards the door before her mother could give her consent. Thankfully, she had donned a pretty yellow walking dress that morning, and apart from briefly waiting for her maid to join her, nothing else delayed her. She ran and fetched her parasol, calling for her abigail.

Bessie, her abigail, had been with her for years, and she was the perfect chaperone. She turned deaf and blind around the couple, discreetly falling back at the right times.

They leisurely set out, enjoying the last few days of sunshine before autumn set in. Summer was over and the season at an end, yet not a cloud dotted the sky.

She stared out at the great expanse, marvelling at the blue that matched her fiancé's eyes.

The Earl spoke cheerfully, "Forgive me, I was out of temper the last time we met."

"It was nothing," Emma replied.

The Earl had expected an apology in return. He waited a moment to see if she would say anything else, and when she remained silent, he wisely did not push the issue. Instead, he smiled, appreciating her good mood, his heart brimming full of plans that he wanted to share with her.

"When do you leave for the Duke's estate?"

Emma turned to face him, looking anxious as she replied, "In a week, and I am not sure how long I will have to stay to convince him. It could be a month or more. My parents have decided to remain in London instead of leaving for our country home. They want to be prepared in case the Duke agrees to a shorter engagement, and London has the best of shops."

"Excellent!" The Earl rubbed his hands together with relish.

Emma stopped walking and planted her hands on her hips. "Do you have a mistress tucked away that I should know about?"

"Eh?"

"The prospect of not seeing me, possibly for months, seems to give you immense pleasure, My Lord."

"Oh, Em, you do not understand. I have a plan. Oh, yes, a most excellent plan."

Emma stared at the Earl. He looked like a little boy who had something awfully naughty up his sleeve. She waited in silence for an explanation. She would hear it, and then decide if she should, in fact, be offended.

He caught her hand and turned to face her, "We just got engaged, and I can't bear to part from you for any length of time. Do you feel the same?"

"Yes," she said slowly, wondering where this was going. "So what is your plan?"

"All this morning I have been investigating, and it seems the Duke needs a head gardener rather desperately. You, my dear, will forge your father's handwriting and write to the Duke. You are to write that a man with the greenest thumb in all of England needs to find an adequate position and would the Duke be willing to hire him."

Emma gaped at him. He could not possibly intend to do what she thought he was intending. Could he?

He eagerly continued, "I have studied botany, so I know a little about plants. I will pretend to be a head gardener, and I wager your wonderful Duke will be none the wiser."

"You are mad. You will be caught in a day."

"I will not be caught, I assure you. We will have more time to spend together," he finished triumphantly.

"Your plan has so many holes that I do not know where to start."

"It does not. Name one."

"What if your plan does work and we marry, how are you to explain posing as his gardener?"

"The Duke does not have time to deal with gardeners. I may see him briefly during his walks. Other than that, he will never know who I am. A person sees what he means to see. If he sees a man dressed as a gardener, then he will look no further."

"He never forgets a face. You do not know him. This plan will never work. The housekeeper does most of the hiring . . . but she has a soft spot for good looking men . . . The Duke is another matter, though . . . This is the most ridiculous plan I have ever heard!"

"Think of our trysts in the garden. The secret meetings would create the perfect scene for courting. The stolen kisses and the scent of danger," he whispered.

Emma coloured up. "If we are caught?"

"That's the genius of the plan, Em. If we are caught, then all will be known, and the result would be that I would have to marry you as soon as possible in case I had compromised you. And that is exactly what we both want," he finished gleefully.

She grinned in return. Her fiancé had a devil of a sense of humour. His plan sounded more and more probable.

"What do I win if you lose the wager?"

"If the Duke discovers me within a month then you, my dear, have permission to follow the Duke's advice on any matter, while my own words can be overlooked. I shall be humbled. What more could you want?"

"And if you win?"

"If I last a month without being discovered, I will confess to your family that I have compromised you. After that, my dear, it will be only a matter of time before a special license is speedily arranged and we are married."

"You are evil you know?"

"I know," he said cheerfully.

"Wait . . . what if the Duke wrote to my father about the gardener, thanking him and such?"

"Mention to the Duke that of late your father has become absent-minded due to the stress of planning the impending wedding and your mother is driving him demented. If your father does reply saying he never sent any gardener, then the Duke can chalk it down to stress. Besides, you can vouch for me, since I will be accompanying you on your journey."

"You have an answer for everything."

The Earl smiled and pulled her into an alcove.

"So you will write the letter?"

"Yes, this sounds like too much fun to disagree."

"That's my brave, Em," he said before bending to kiss her.

Chapter 3

Emma was convinced she had lost her mind. What in the world had possessed her to agree to the Earl's plan? He had been standing too close to her, and his talk of kisses and trysts had addled her brain.

How could she have thought, even for a moment, that having the Earl disguise himself as the Duke's gardener would be fun? What in the world were they thinking?

She sat on her bed staring at the letter she had just written to the Duke. She had to admit that her forgery was pretty convincing.

She was used to corresponding with her father's associates when he was busy, and copying his handwriting had seemed entertaining a few years ago. Practice had improved her skills, and she had even written to the Duke at times when her father wished it. The Duke had never been able to tell the difference.

She was not worried about being found out. The letter would not pose an issue, rather it was the Earl that worried her.

If the Earl had thought her brothers were bad, then the Duke was far worse.

The Duke had one daughter called Catherine whom she was very close to. This closeness had led them to spend a lot of time together over the years. So much so that the Duke had become extremely fond of her and begun treating her like a second daughter.

However, his fondness translated to running her life as well as his daughter's. He could be most generous, but in return, he expected complete obedience. It was a marvel he had agreed to the wedding at all.

Sighing she set aside the letter. She wondered if she should post it or hand it over to the Duke when she met him. Giving it to him personally seemed the safer option. The post was unreliable, and hopefully this way he would not feel obligated to reply to her father.

She stretched her toes seeking the warmth of hot bricks. Bessie had forgotten them again.

She shivered in her shift and wrapped the quilt tighter around herself. Her thoughts once again flowed back to the Earl.

He thought this was all a game. He seemed to overlook the fact that he would have to sleep in the servant quarters and deal with people not of his class.

Did he even know what a head gardener's duties entailed? Would he even last a week? She did not think so. A part of her wanted to keep him close by . . . but considering the risk it was better he didn't stay too long.

If her uncle discovered the deceit, then there would be hell to pay. The Duke would not blame her parents for her folly, but he could make life exceedingly difficult for them nonetheless.

What could she do, she wondered, biting her lip. Dissuading the Earl was impossible. She had no choice. She would have to wait and see how things played out.

❖ ❖ ❖

The Earl had not been this happy or excited since the time he had been a student. The social whirlwind irked him, and the last few years of the same old rigmarole had been unbearable.

It wasn't that he disliked the company. It was the rules of the ton that chafed at him. And a chance to get away from it all was simply wonderful.

Hence, he threw himself into creating the perfect image of a gardener. The head gardener could not be a young man, so his excellent valet had procured some beards and moustaches of all shades and sizes.

The Earl eagerly tried one after the other until he found the perfect one.

His clothes had to be appropriate. He wondered if adding a walking stick and a clay pipe was too much. He decided to keep the clay pipe. He was not a good actor, his honest face showing far more than he liked. Hence, the need for a prop. He could puff away when he wanted to avoid answering a question or pretend to fill it to buy time.

Except his valet, no one would be aware of his real identity. This was his chance to be free and do as he pleased. As an Earl with a large, flourishing estate, he had to be responsible and project a certain image.

He could not afford to have his workers find him in his cups, dancing au naturel in the streets. He could no longer cavort with the local wenches or try and spike his great aunt Agatha's drink just to hear her croon bawdy songs in the village church. Those days were long gone.

Yet, now he had a chance to throw off his aristocratic mantle and live life the way he wanted to.

Four long weeks of sheer pleasure and freedom awaited him.

Smiling, he ordered his valet to carefully pack his bags and add nothing of value, not even his expensive tobacco. The scent could alert anyone, and the Earl wanted to do things right.

His persona would be perfect, from the top of his powdered hair to the dirt artfully added under his toenails.

❖ ❖ ❖

Over the next few days, Emma tried to convince the Earl to give up the entire foolish escapade. This was not a play but real life, where if things went wrong, the result could be disastrous.

The Earl assumed Emma had no faith in his skills or his intelligence; hence, his need to prove her wrong grew stronger day by day, and soon whatever iota of doubt that had remained in him vanished in response to Emma's scepticism.

"We leave at eight in the morning tomorrow," Emma said grudgingly.

"Who will be accompanying you?" the Earl asked.

"My maid Bessie, a few male servants for our safety . . . " She paused and added slyly, "and my mother . . . who will stay with us for an entire week."

"You never mentioned your mother's stay before?"

Emma noted that the Earl did not look agitated at the news. He had been expecting something of the sort.

"I may have pushed her a little bit. After all, I will not have much time to spend with her once I am married," she said defensively.

"To discourage me and foil our plans before we even start," the Earl remarked shrewdly.

"Did it work?" she asked hopefully.

"On the contrary, my dear, it will allow me to travel in leisure and see to decent accommodations for my valet, as he will be staying in the village nearby. You have been most unhelpful in answering my queries regarding the Duke except to say he is wonderful. It will give me a chance to investigate a little. Servants at times know a lot more, and they talk."

"He will be suspicious as to your identity if you arrive after us. He may decide to investigate. I mean, he is a cautious man, and he couldn't be sure that you are not an imposter who has done away with the real gardener to steal the family jewels. Once he finds you have no history except my father to recommend you, he will ferret you out before you even start work."

"My dear, I will not be found out. He can investigate to his heart's content. My head gardener retired a year ago, and I have adopted his complete persona. If the Duke does try and investigate, then he will write to me to clarify as his previous employer. I will give the man a glowing recommendation, since he was a truly excellent gardener. My valet will keep me up to date about letters and such. The gardener now lives in a remote village, and except for me and my valet, no one has bothered to learn of his whereabouts. I will also confirm, should the Duke ask, that I had recommended the man to your father, since he wanted to live in the country. The London air was depressing the man, and I could not see a faithful employee suffer so."

"How can he know that you recommended him to Father? Father is unaware of our charade, remember?" she said triumphantly.

"That is where you come in. You will steal all the letters the Duke writes to your father and reply to them if needed. You can reply to the letter and say that I recommended the gardener."

Emma glared at him. "I will do no such thing. What of my poor delicate nerves? They would never be able to handle the suspense."

The Earl laughed outright at that.

Emma left him spluttering in mirth while she made her way home. She had a lot to finish before the day was over, and she had done her duty in warning him.

He could behave like a child and play games if he wanted to. She was washing her hands off the entire affair. Feeling calmer once the decision was made, she went about her day in a much better mood.

❖ ❖ ❖

The Earl had all his gardeners lined up in a row.

They watched him nervously. The last time the Earl had requested their presence had been to conduct an experiment.

He had just begun studying medicine at the university, and botany happened to be an important part of his studies. He had requested the gardeners to provide him with certain varieties of herbs.

He had then pounded, poured, strained, and mixed together various tinctures. The gardeners had been bid to drink the various multihued liquids.

The poor fellows drank the proffered concoctions and gave their names to be written on the labels of bottles that they had partaken of.

The results were duly noted by the Earl and were the following:

Gardener one – Excessive gas – Was thrown out of bed by his wife for three days straight.

Gardener two – Skin has turned an unsightly orange – May have a remedy, though the deuced man runs every time he sees me.

Gardener three – His face seems to have taken on a queer visage. It looks like tiny fish with extremely sharp teeth have made a feast of him.

Gardener four – Has not yet emerged from the privy.

Gardener five – Could have given the man the pox.

. . . And on the list went. Twenty gardeners had avoided the Earl for the next five years. This was the first time they had been called to his presence once more. As he was the Earl now, they had no choice but to comply.

The Earl was sympathetic as their nervousness was understandable.

"Now, I have not asked you here to conduct any sort of experimentation," he said soothingly.

They did not look convinced and eyed him warily.

"I simply need a list of your duties and a few hours of your time. I want to learn a little bit about what you do."

The faces changed to alarm. Did the Earl doubt their expertise? Was he planning to let some of them go? Was he in some sort of financial trouble?

The Earl continued, "The reason I want to know a bit about the sort of work you do is because I intend to have a patch of my own. I find myself drawn to the magic of plants. I want to see them grow and nurture them as they bear fruits. It is a beautiful hobby to have, and I request your help."

The gardeners eyed him sceptically. They had heard of ladies tending to flower patches. Head gardeners all over England had a devil of a job sneaking to the chosen garden plot and fixing the disaster that had been unleashed upon the plants.

The ladies, in turn, believed the health of their beautiful blooms lay fully in their own green hands. While they boasted to fellow ladies of their accomplishments in their latest hobby, the poor gardener sweated and toiled to keep up such appearances.

If his interests were encouraged, the Earl would be a terror. Silently, the men vowed to deter the Earl from choosing any such leisure activity.

In the end, they gave him a highly exaggerated account of all that was involved.

The Earl dismissed the men and sat down to think. He, as the head gardener, would be required to tend to the most sensitive plants. He had to inspect the entire estate for plant diseases, destructive insects, weeds, and fruit-eating birds.

He was also responsible for under-gardeners numbering twenty to forty, depending on the size of the estate. He had to resolve petty disputes, provide the kitchens, keep account of fruits and vegetables, and ensure the flowers bloomed when they should and not a minute sooner. It was a daunting task, to say the least, and he wanted to give up there and then.

A vision of Emma rose before his eyes, bringing his negative thoughts to a screeching halt.

He was no coward, and a few sprigs of grass would not keep him away from attempting this charade. He could always delegate, after all, and everyone under him knew what to do. He may not know as much as a gardener would about soil and seeds, but he did know something of politics.

Chapter 4

"You any good with 'em plants? The Duke doesn't hire riff raffs mind you."

"Some say I am a doctor of plants. My roses are the finest and the fruits I grow, the sweetest."

"Hear this lads, he says he is the doctor of plants. You take 'em and put their broken branches up in slings and dose 'em with some Laudanum, eh?"

"Mayhap you sing the wee ones some lullaby!"

The pub roared with laughter while the Earl scowled through his beard.

He had expected the dirty mugs and the flea infested bed, but he had not expected to become the butt of all jokes.

It had all started with choosing the wrong sort of name. He should have chosen some other gardener to impersonate, but his own retired man had seemed so perfect. He was conveniently far away with no one aware of his whereabouts.

He had often wondered at the fierce expression on his gardener's face every time he had encountered him. Lord or lowly servant would be all treated to that same angry expression. He scared the maids and terrified the housekeeper.

Had he not been such a wonderful gardener the Earl would have let him go. Instead, he had worked for him until the ripe old age of sixty.

The Earl felt a twinge of sympathy for the old man. He no longer blamed the man for his severe visage, since he was doing a darned good imitation of it at that moment.

His plan had worked beautifully up until the time they had taken up lodgings at the inn nearby the Duke's residence.

Every time he was introduced, the game of let's pull the new gardener's leg began. He could hardly hold a decent conversation for more than a minute before striding out in anger.

His valet had proved to be a treasure since his own investigations were coming to naught. Burns, with his perfectly respectable name, had gone out to glean what information he could.

"Why are we packing, Burns?"

"Sir, we are going back to London."

The Earl took out his snow-white handkerchief and placed it on a chair. He then perched his bottom carefully on the cloth. Once done, he turned back to his valet, whose countenance resembled the peeling yellow walls.

"And why are we going back?"

"Sir, that man, the Duke, is a terror. The last time he caught a man trying to cheat him he made him wear his housekeeper's skirts, sat him on a donkey, and took him for a ride around the village."

"Hmm"

"My Lord, they . . . the little girls . . . they threw flowers at him."

"Stop trembling. He wouldn't dare do that to an Earl."

"The man who cheated him had been a baron."

The Earl gulped. The valet resumed packing.

"This is the test of true love, Burns. The Duke is my personal dragon, standing in the way of my claiming the beautiful princess. I will not allow him to kidnap my beautiful Emma, even if it means facing my death."

"Sir, didn't she go to him on her own?"

"Dash it, you fail to see the romance of it all."

"After ten years of being married to my missus, forgive me for forgetting what romance is like," Burns retorted.

This entire business of telling Burns to treat him as an equal was simply not working out. He had wanted to get into character and had threatened and cajoled his valet to speak his mind. Now that Burns was getting into the spirit of things, the Earl was not feeling particularly happy.

"We are not leaving before the month is over, and that is the end of it. Unpack the bags," he ordered.

Burns stood looking torn. His full red cheeks puffed in agitation. He finally sighed and did as he was told.

The Earl gave a sharp nod and after checking his appearance in the dirty, cracked mirror nailed to the wall, he proceeded to the

Duke's estate.

❖ ❖ ❖

"It is difficult to decide what to do?"

The Earl stared at Mrs Purcell nervously. She had to hire him; he couldn't have it otherwise. The woman standing before him was tall and thin faced, just the type he would have imagined the Duke to hire — capable and cold.

"What may be the problem, Miss? Is something out of order?"

"I received instructions from the Duke, and you come highly recommended. You seem to know your plants."

The Earl certainly hoped so. With his years spent studying botany amongst other subjects at Oxford, he had better know his roots from his shoots.

Not to mention the entire day he had spent toiling in his own field being instructed by ten terribly boisterous and contradictory gardeners.

She frowned. "It is your name. How am I supposed to call out to you? It will not do for a lady to utter such a name. Even writing it down in the books would be mortifying, especially since the accountant goes over them."

A prude as well, thought the Earl agitatedly.

He said reassuringly, "It is a common enough name, I assure you, miss."

"Yes, well, that may be so, but I don't have people with such names in my employ."

The Earl remained silent, cursing his beard and his filthy clothes. Getting people to do what he wanted had always been easy for him. He simply charmed them with his looks. Being without his title was suddenly making him realise how vulnerable he truly was.

He wondered how people managed daily without any assets. Every day would be a struggle if one always had to depend on one's wit rather than one's looks or name.

Mrs Purcell tapped her feet thoughtfully. "We have been waiting for over two months for a head gardener. I have been searching high and low. There is such a dearth of reliable servants these days. And I simply cannot have the gardens neglected much longer. The under-gardeners are decent lads who know their job, but they have been constantly bickering with one another. Each one is trying to vie for the position of the head gardener and wanting to do their own thing.

I cannot have roses growing in the patch of daisies, and I do not have the time to deal with petty rivalries. I am at my wits end, so to speak . . . And as I have no choice at the moment, I will take you on. Mind you, it will be a temporary position until I find someone to replace you . . . unless you intend to change your name?"

"I have borne this name for over sixty years, madam. Why, my father and his grandfather and his grandfather had all been named thus. It is the matter of my roots, and each one of us has succeeded in creating the most magnificent gardens. My ancestor was an under-gardener to the English King's head gardener himself. I do not like to boast, but . . . ."

"Yes, yes, that is enough," said Mrs Purcell hurriedly. She realised he was one of those long-winded types. The older a man got, the wordier he seemed to get.

"Is that all, Mrs Purcell? May I start work in the morning?"

"Yes, you can come to the kitchens at nine, and you will be shown your accommodations and things."

The Earl waited, knowing she would have to say it.

"Thank you . . . err . . . Mr . . , err . . . Shufflebottom."

The Earl left, still chuckling into his sleeve.

❖ ❖ ❖

It had been over a week, and Emma was wondering where the Earl had got to. He had not even written to her.

She did not like feeling worried, and it was an odd sensation worrying about someone's safety other than one's own immediate family. She already missed him terribly.

Maybe he had decided to stay in London and give up the whole foolish charade. Curiously that made her feel disappointed. In spite of all her arguments, she had looked forward to the grand scheme.

She glanced back at her maid and her cousin strolling slowly behind her. Emma enjoyed a good brisk walk, while her abigail was too fat to keep up. Her slim cousin liked to amble leisurely, most of the time her head was lost in some book or the other that she was reading.

It was difficult to force her cousin outdoors, and she worried about her coming out next year . . . her reverie was interrupted by a hiss.

"Psst."

Emma started. She peered at the apple trees. The sound had been loud, but she couldn't see anyone close by.

"This way."

Emma turned to her right and made her way towards the bit where the trees grew closer together. As soon as she was hidden from the main path, she felt a hand clasp around her mouth.

"Hush, don't scream. It is me, Richard."

Emma nodded, her eyes wide. The moment he took his hands off her, she dissolved into giggles.

The Earl, who had once been the epitome of high fashion, bordering on being a fop, was now clad in a set of dirty shirt and trousers. He wore a long, full beard with a moustache to rival, and his hair was powdered white. To complete the look he had blackened a few of his teeth and reeked of some cheap tobacco.

"I don't think I want to kiss you, My Lord."

The Earl smiled ruefully. "I did not think so. Now, listen quickly before your maid catches up. I have procured the post of the head gardener, and I am now living in the servants' quarters. I need to see you again. We have to find a way of occasionally meeting without anyone being around. I cannot come to you or send a message, so you will have to plan the means."

"Well done, Richard. I will try and meet you in the gardens tomorrow morning. My maid likes to sleep in, so I often slip out without waking her. I usually never do that in the Duke's household, but since you have taken such a risk, then I can too." She paused, and then asked cheekily, "Should I count today as the start of the wager?"

"Well . . . I began work this morning . . . so yes, you may mark your calendar. Shall I see you at six? Or is that too early? Most of the household would be indoors at that time."

"Six is fine. If I need to send a message, who do I ask for?"

"Shufflebottom"

The Earl left his fiancée in peals of laughter as he hobbled his way back to the gardens.

Chapter 5

"Emma?" Lady Catherine Arden, the Duke's only child, called out.

Emma stifled her giggles and turned to face her cousin.

"What are you laughing about?" Catherine asked.

Emma's eyes danced. "I saw an uncommonly large squirrel being outwitted by a clever, scrawny one. It was quite entertaining."

Catherine eyed her cousin sceptically. Sometimes Emma had an imagination that rivalled her books. "We must turn back. It is almost time for tea, and you know how Father despises tardiness."

Emma's smile was replaced by a scowl. She had forgotten how strict her uncle was. Her pleasure in meeting her cousin had pushed all negative aspects of staying at Arden Estates to the back of her mind. "How do you live with him every single day? So many rules, and that boring chaperone!"

Catherine shrugged. "It's not so bad. I guess I have not known any different, so it is easier for me than it is for you. Aunty takes some getting used to, though. I would have asked my father for another duenna, but she is, after all, his sister. I couldn't hurt her feelings."

"You are far too soft-hearted. Lady Babbage is the worst of her kind. She would, if she could, create a shrine for her needles and pray before it. All she ever does is sew and expects us to do the same. She refuses to venture out, and that is simply not fair to you. How are you meant to socialise if she keeps you cooped up indoors? It's unfortunate enough that the Duke would not let you come out until you are twenty. Twenty is too late. I think . . . I think he is afraid you will marry and leave him alone. His love for you is suffocating."

Catherine turned and started walking back. She slipped an arm through Emma's to show she was not angry. "I don't think I will have trouble finding a man when I do come out," she said smiling.

"The Duke's daughter and beautiful," Emma nodded. "I, for one, am glad you stayed hidden away in the country. One look at you and the Earl would have never looked at me twice."

"I think my finding a man will depend more on my status rather than my looks. It will be an arranged marriage, and I don't think father will have it any other way."

"You underestimate yourself. You always have. You will be the diamond of the first water, mark my words. I, for one, wish I had your golden hair and bright blue eyes."

"While I wish I had your dark curls and witchy green eyes," replied Catherine grinning.

The mansion loomed up ahead. It was a dark, forbidding structure that rambled and stretched as far as the eye could see. The deep grey stone walls did not look so ominous in the daylight, but Emma was aware that within a few hours, when the sun started sinking, it would be swathed in shadows. At night, the long carpeted hallways would fail to muffle the creaks of aged floorboards, and certain doors would grate as they were opened. As soon as October set in, the house would truly shudder and creak. The wind wailing and banging on the windows would find an open crack and whistle through the house like a banshee.

Emma silently thanked the bright sun for diminishing her childish fears.

They made their way inside and had just enough time to change out of their walking clothes before the bell was rung.

Emma entered the family room and found everyone seated in their usual places.

Lady Babbage sat in the far corner almost hidden by the curtains. She seemed to fade into the background, and one often forgot when she was in the room. She never said anything witty, and her chatter was so monotonous that people, in general, avoided saying more than two words to her.

She sat knitting something blue, wearing a brown dress that blended into the deep gold brocade curtains behind her. Her beady eyes blinked as she peered at Emma. Her round face broke into a smile, and she nodded enthusiastically.

Emma returned the smile and quickly turned away. She made her way towards the Duchess and Catherine, who sat together on the fraud.

The Duke's eyes stayed on his face a little too long before he turned away.

"Emma, walk with me."

Emma glanced at the Earl nervously and then followed the Duke. She could do nothing else.

"Emma, have you seen that gardener before?"

Emma took a moment to answer. "Uncle, I . . . that is, mother and I had visited the Earl at his home in London. He had been entertaining his sister at the time, and I had noticed the gardener. I did not recall him until he mentioned working for the Earl just now."

"I see. Why were you walking about alone?"

"I woke early, and sometimes I like to walk before breakfast. My maid felt out of sorts, so I let her sleep. I did not have the heart to disturb Lady Babbage."

"Next time, Emma, stay indoors unless you have a suitable chaperone."

"Yes, uncle," she replied quietly.

He could have been extremely angry, but his mind seemed preoccupied. She wondered uneasily if the Earl had made him suspicious. The Duke would have to investigate now, and that meant she would have to go through his letters and make sure the Earl's secret stayed safe.

Emma silently cursed the Earl and his foolish babbling. It was hard to hide his upbringing, and he had not had enough time to prepare his accent. Still, this was his own foolish plan to begin with.

Oh! Why did he have to spout Latin now of all times?

Chapter 6

"You seem disturbed, my dear, is anything the matter?"

Emma looked at Lady Babbage in surprise. She had never expected the woman to be so perceptive. Even Catherine was unaware of the turmoil raging inside her.

She was worried about the Earl, and she was sure the Duke would start his investigations soon. She would have to steal into his study and go over his letters. She could not afford to have the Duke delving into the head gardener's background by writing to Bow Street Runners or private investigators.

Her father's denials of sending a gardener could no longer be waived off either. Richard would receive any correspondence written to him, but the entire scene of the morning might prompt the Duke not to trust him.

This charade was getting harder by the day and the lies piling up.

Emma forced her features to relax as she answered Lady Babbage. "No, I am alright. I woke Early this morning, so I am a trifle tired."

"Are you sure there is nothing else bothering you? You can trust an old woman, and I am hardly a gossip. Perhaps I can help?"

"I assure you, it is nothing, Lady Babbage."

Lady Babbage searched Emma's face and shook her head dissatisfied. She leaned over and patted her hand.

Emma was touched by the woman's concern. She may have judged the woman harshly. She was boring, one could not get away from that fact, but she was kind as well. Emma gave her a genuine smile for the first time.

She was wrong about Catherine not noticing her distress. As soon as Catherine got Emma alone, she asked her what was wrong.

Emma had the urge to spill all her secrets. But she had given her word to the Earl, and Catherine may not find the entire thing as entertaining as she hoped. They were, after all, lying to her father. On the other hand, Catherine would be right in scolding her, since deceiving the Duke was no longer fun.

"I must be missing Richard," Emma murmured. It was partly true.

Catherine accepted her statement, confident Emma would not hide anything from her.

"The Barkers arrived this afternoon. Mamma put them up in the guest rooms. They have been resting from the long journey and will join us for dinner."

Emma's mood grew more depressed. "Oh, can we not send them back?"

"I don't think we can put frogs in Prudence's bed anymore. We have no choice but to behave like well-bred women and let them stay as long as they like." She was quiet for a moment and then continued, "I don't understand why Father says Sir Henry Barker is his good friend. I have never seen them have a meaningful conversation, and I doubt the Barkers have an ounce of intelligence between them to excite any interest in Father."

Emma glanced at Catherine. She had never heard her cousin speak ill of anyone before. What had prompted that anger on her face?

Catherine continued in a low, agitated tone. "This last one year when you left for London I realised that we had grown up. I could no longer afford to have my head in the clouds. I started observing people to get over my shyness. Once you know something intimately, then you lose your fear of it. I am still learning and do not pretend to be an expert on human behaviour. Since I have always been so quiet and lost, it is easier for people who know me to let down their guard. I watched Mrs Barker today when they arrived. You were taking a nap at the time, and I had gone to the library to fetch a book. What I saw made me realise that some people are truly vicious."

"What did you see?"

"I may be reading too much into it, and I don't want to tell you lest it colours your perception as well. Just observe her today at dinner, and see if you notice anything odd. Try and forget her grating voice, and for once listen to all she has to say. I would like your opinion before being entirely convinced that I am right."

Emma searched her cousin's face thoughtfully. She recalled the last time Prudence had joined them for an extended stay. She had been a pest, making Catherine her target. She would pick faults and criticize everything Cat did, often running to the Duke with nasty tales. She did not dare offend Emma because she knew Emma would not tolerate it and would reciprocate in kind.

During the entire time that Prudence had stayed with them, Catherine maintained her good humour. Yet now, within a day of their arrival, her cousin looked decidedly vexed.

Mrs Barker had always seemed flighty like her daughter. She was foolish yet harmless, so hearing her angelic cousin describe Mrs Barker as vicious was astonishing, to say the least.

Emma was secretly delighted to see that something could ruffle her cousin's composure, though she wasn't sure if she should get enjoyment from something like this. Her own troubles seemed less severe, and the prospect of entertainment instead of a painful dinner had her back in good humour.

❖ ❖ ❖

The Earl was still growling in frustration. Every few minutes the entire encounter with the Duke would rise before his eyes and mock him. Very clever, he thought to himself irritably. Babble like a fool in front of the Duke to impress Emma. That was exactly what he was here for, to make a complete and utter goose of himself and make the Duke look grander than King George.

He should pack his bags and return to his home in London. He was a pathetic excuse of an Earl, and all his fancy schooling was more of a hindrance than a help. No matter how hard he tried, his lofty accents refuse to change into cruder tones of a commoner. That was another reason why the other servants made fun of him.

The only pleasure he got were the few minutes stolen at his valet's rooms where he ordered a bath and soaked himself to the bone. Constantly bending over flower beds and stooping was making him feel as old as the gardener he was impersonating. He slipped deeper into the warm tub, wriggling his toes in pleasure.

His ego was thoroughly bruised. In fact, it had been trampled on, and heels had been dug in the particularly sore spots, over and over again.

He recalled a horrid time in his life when he had last felt this lost amongst strangers. He had been ten years old at the time. His mother had hugged him tight and bawled all over his new shirt before dropping him off at a prestigious boarding school, aptly named, 'The Austere Academy for Gentlemen'.

His father had firmly told him that this would be his new home for a while. Yet, his young mind had refused to grasp the fact that after a day of playing with children his own age he would not be going home for the night. He had assumed his parents had been jesting.

By supper time, he was fed up. After being served a sorry soup, soggy bread, and the worst tasting rice pudding in all of England, the young Earl could handle no more.

He threw down his spoons and let out an outraged howl. He no longer cared if the other boys thought he was a baby for crying. He bawled and cried, but no one seemed in the least interested. He was petted by a teacher but told firmly that he would have to stay. The Earl took this as a challenge. The gauntlet had been thrown.

His full-throated cry had set off a number of youngsters, and while the teachers rushed to soothe the many screaming children, the Earl brushed off his tears and stood up. He squared his shoulders and slowly made his way towards the door. He gripped the brass handle with his small, greasy hands and twisted with all his might. The door groaned open, and he was off like a shot, making his way towards the main entrance. He was out in the gardens before the teachers realised what had happened.

The guards noticed the Earl running out of the gate and attempted to stop the young lad.

The Earl, using all his wiles, dodged the guards. He leaped into the air, somersaulted twice and rolled on the ground at a speed of an over excited cricket ball. He dived under the arms of the guards and skidded between their legs on his way to freedom.

He had a good start, and some students emboldened by the sight of the running Earl, joined him in his cause.

The teachers ran helter-skelter catching boys of various sizes, and in the confusion the Earl cleverly climbed up an apple tree on the outskirts of the school. He sat munching a juicy apple while the entire school came out with torches to hunt down the deserter.

The dark worked to his advantage. The Earl was not discovered. He slipped down the tree when he deemed it safe and made his way towards the main road. He used his pocket money to hitch a ride to his home four hours away from the school.

His pitiful allowance would not have gotten him so far, but the old farmer had a soft heart. He had luckily been going that very route, and carrying the little tear stained boy would not put him out. He gently wrapped a blanket around the boy and tucked him in at the back of the cart.

The Earl slept peacefully and only woke to his mother's horrified screeches.

He was deposited back to the school within two days. Yet, his success in outwitting the entire school had made him a hero amongst the other boys. They looked at him in admiration.

His brilliant ideas of gluing teachers to chairs, putting spiders in desks and bribing servants for treats, to name a few, bought him the loyalty and love of his classmates.

When he grew a little older, his status as the heir to the Hamilton estate and Earldom won him the respect of his peers. Apart from his standing in society, the Earl's very nature endeared him to those around him. His affability, charm and his ever ready spark of mischief made it hard for others not to genuinely like him. Except for the occasional bouts of fisticuffs that were considered normal for any growing healthy boy, the Earl led an easy life.

That easy life continued until he turned eighteen, after which his parents died.

They had been traveling to Africa, and their ship was caught in a storm and sank at sea. That was when he started learning about responsibilities, but even then he had been treated well by his peers.

Never in his life had he been teased so mercilessly. Someone who had grown up with taunts might have had a better time of it. They would have become immune to it, learnt to ignore the jibes or laugh it off.

The Earl was unaware of how to react, and his angry outbursts delighted and encouraged his bullies. Living the life of a servant was dreary, and they found what joy they could in their games, however, petty or cruel.

Not everyone treated him badly he acknowledged. The cook always kept the softest meat for him so his old teeth would not suffer. The housekeeper kept a polite, respectful distance, and the under gardeners did not dare cross him as he was the one in charge.

However, the stable hands, Pickering the butler and the various other helpers around the estate had no qualms about taking pleasure in his annoyance.

The Earl seethed quietly. He truly did not want to stay on any longer. Yet, perversely, he wanted see the charade through until the end and win this game. He was not a coward or a quitter. Once he made up his mind, he always stuck to his decision with bull-headed doggedness.

He decided that he would start by taking risks. The Duke could discover his identity at any time, and he no longer had the leisure to take things slow.

He would have his fun, since that was exactly why he had started this whole thing in the first place. He could always escape before the Duke put him up on a donkey in a lady's skirt.

A slow smile spread across his face as he planned his next move.

"You are rapidly resembling a dried grape, My Lord."

The Earl grinned as he stepped out of the tub. He wanted to get right back to the Arden estate and put his plans into action.

Chapter 7

Emma walked into the dining room and was momentarily stunned speechless. The guests were already seated, but she wished they hadn't been . . .

Mrs Barker had her assets spilling out of her scarlet gown, and a hysterical Emma wondered if the footman could balance the soup plate on the gigantic breasts on display. Her upright position gave her a splendid view down the never-ending depths of Mrs Barker's ample bosom.

She hurried to take her seat beside Catherine.

They caught each other's eyes and stifled a giggle. Catherine discreetly tilted her head towards her right. Emma glanced in the direction indicated and once more forced her open mouth to close.

Prudence Barker sat in a deep pink gown, wearing a hairdo that rivalled the Tower of London. Emma could scarcely see the hovering servant behind the pile of curls. A massive teapot was placed carefully in the nest of black curls.

"That is an interesting hairstyle, Prudence," remarked the Duchess. Even she had been brought out of her haze by the extraordinary vision.

"It is, isn't it? It is all the rage in France. Why, the Countess of Elridge, who as we all know is the very epitome of fashion, had a ship perched atop her head. It is difficult to move one's head lest the tea dribble down and ruins one's dress, but I think I have mastered the art," replied Prudence, pink with pleasure at the thought of creating such a stir.

"Surely you do not need to fill the teapot with tea? It is not as if you are going to drink it, since it must be stone cold by now. And getting it out of your hair must be a task in itself," commented the Duke blandly.

"Oh, but if one does something, then one must do it right," chirped Mrs Barker. "My daughter has been out long enough to know what is deemed proper," she finished, glancing meaningfully at Catherine.

Catherine, to give her credit, did not change colour but smiled back amiably. Her own hair was brushed back into an elegant, low coif.

They paused briefly while the soup was served. Once the servers departed, Mrs Barker leaned forward and once again addressed the Duke, "I did not want to wear such a bold colour tonight, Your Grace. I mean," she said simpering, "I am too old to wear such things, but Poo Poo positively insisted. She would have it no other way."

Emma mouthed 'Poo Poo' to Catherine, who promptly disappeared under the table pretending to retrieve a fallen fork. Her shoulders shook alarmingly in silent laughter, and Emma had a hard time not joining her.

The Duke could not but help peek at the aforementioned dress. That had been the lady's intent all along. He quickly looked away and clearing his throat said, "It is a . . . flattering colour, and you are not so old yet, Mrs Barker."

"I feel miles better now that you have stated you approve. I was terribly worried about being inappropriate in your household, but now I may wear such colours without any qualms," Mrs Barker tittered.

Emma dug her nails into her palm. It was not the colour that was inappropriate, as the lady well knew, but the cut of the dress.

"I must warn you, Mrs Barker," commented the Duchess. The words had the effect of stopping all spoons in mid-air.

"Warn me?" asked Mrs Barker nervously.

"Why, yes, my dear. I have already told the rest present here, and because you are living with us as a guest, I have a duty to inform you of the danger."

Emma relaxed back in her seat and continued eating.

"What sort of danger?" Mrs Barker asked irritably.

"This house has passed into a phase where spirits walk. The walls thrum with danger, and the departed wish us to be forewarned. A catastrophe is to occur soon, and I am afraid you are now in the midst of it. You can depart if you wish, we will not hold it against you."

Emma wanted to laugh. The Duchess was obviously trying to send Mrs Barker packing the only way she could. She noticed Catherine controlling her smile as well.

"Thank you for your concern, Your Grace, but as good friends of the family, it would hardly do for us to leave you in the midst of danger. I think you would need all the help you can get, so we shall stay," said Mr Barker to everyone's surprise.

He was normally a silent man who was more interested in his port than making conversation. So the strength in his voice insisting that they stay on had the effect of making everyone thoughtful. Even Mrs Barker looked disconcerted.

"You are welcome to stay as long as you like, no matter the circumstances," the Duke said, shooting his wife a quelling look.

"Thank you, you always make us feel most welcome," Mrs Barker replied, stressing the last word unnecessarily.

This time the innuendo in her tone was clear to all, except perhaps the Duchess, who was busy having a one-sided conversation with an invisible, dead ancestor.

"This duck is lovely. I must get the recipe for the sauce," said Lady Babbage into the uncomfortable silence.

No one pointed out that since Lady Babbage lived with the Duke and intended to live with him until her dying day, she did not need to know the recipe. Nor did anyone point out that the duck was, in fact, chicken.

Everyone spoke at once, grasping the topic of food and spent the next few minutes debating the flavour of lamb versus beef and who preferred what. They had assumed that Mrs Barker would give up after the awkward moment, but they failed to remember exactly how dim she truly was.

She waved a fork with a tomato speared at the end as she spoke, her high voice drowning out everyone else's.

"The food is delicious," she said, licking her lips, "but then you always have the best, Your Grace. I have a mind to stay on forever," she giggled.

The effect was ruined as the tomato dislodged and dropped into the valley of her remarkable bosom. Unfortunately, she did not realise that and wondered what made Emma giggle in merriment. Catherine was not far behind in joining her. The returning servers gave them a moment of respite to calm down.

The meal was finished in a similar vein, leaving the girls angry yet amused. The men stayed on to pass the port, and the ladies retired to the salon.

Catherine went to pour the tea, and Emma followed her. She could not wait until everyone retired for bed to say what she wanted.

"I have never noticed Mrs Barker so desperate. Is it just me or was she outrageously flirting with the Duke?"

"That is exactly what I noticed this afternoon. I am sure she has flirted with him on previous occasions, but this time she is taking it too far. It is embarrassing, and I am surprised Mr Barker does not say anything or, for that matter, the Duke," said Catherine worriedly.

"You must be funning, Cat." Emma searched her cousin's face, and when no dimple winked, she continued, "The Duke would never take her seriously. She made a fool of herself, and you should simply see her as an amusing diversion."

"The Duke is a man, Em, and however much we may dance around the topic, my stepmother is not all there."

Emma placed a hand on Catherine's rigid shoulder. "The Duke is still handsome and extremely powerful. The last person he would turn to would be Mrs Barker. He may want some other diversion, a mistress, perhaps, if he does not have one already. But he will never fall for a woman like her."

"I hope you are right. I suppose I never bothered to think of the effect my stepmother's madness had on my father. I do hope he has someone to love him."

"He has you, and as for female companionship, I don't think it's our place to be concerned."

"I was just taken by surprise, I think. I have never witnessed any woman throwing herself at my father before. He normally shields me from such things."

"Maybe he feels that you are old enough to handle it now, or that you have grown up enough to notice — " She abruptly stopped, her eyes darting towards the door. She urgently squeezed Catherine's arm and muttered, "The men are entering the room. You should go to your father and stick by him for the rest of the evening. Hurry, Cat, he needs to be rescued."

Catherine quickly turned and beat the approaching Mrs Barker by a second. She then spent the night keeping the thankful Duke occupied, while Mrs Barker sulked in annoyance.

❖ ❖ ❖

Emma sent her maid off to bed and sat down to think. She was once again worried about the Duke's suspicions regarding the gardener. The only time she could sneak into his library and go through the papers was when the entire house was asleep. She had undressed so that her maid would not be suspicious.

Now she strode to her closet and pulled out her robe. She was bending over to put on her slippers when a hand was clasped around her mouth.

She was pulled upright, and she instinctively bent her knee and let her foot fly back and ram itself between the legs of the intruder. It was a beautiful move taught to her by her brothers.

A low moan of pain came from behind her and the hands fell away to release her.

She smiled satisfactorily as she turned to look upon the unfortunate creature who had dared to enter her bedchamber.

Chapter 8

"Richard!" Emma gasped.

"Hello darling, I thought it was time I got my kiss. But I think you have permanently damaged the parts that would have one day given you children," he groaned.

"I am so sorry! Are you alright? How did you get in? You can't be here, what if someone finds out?"

"I got in through the door. However romantic I may want to be, I didn't want to risk climbing the ivy and breaking my neck. I didn't realise that walking in through the door would be just as dangerous." He paused to breathe deeply. Clenching his teeth in pain, he continued. "I will be fine . . . at least, I hope I will be in a few days. As for being found out, the entire household is asleep. After the risk I have already taken, this seemed relatively tame."

"You don't have your beard on, and your teeth are white again."

"I did not want to give you an excuse to evade my kiss this time."

Emma blushed. It was different kissing the Earl in the light of the day or even in dark gardens, but his being in her room was disturbing. It somehow felt more intimate, and the fact that no one would intrude on them for some hours had her feeling shy and tensed.

"How . . . how did you know this was my room?"

The Earl smiled, guessing the reason for Emma's discomfort. His kiss would have to wait, and recalling the state he was in, he did not mind delaying it too much.

"It was easy enough. All I had to do was follow your maid Bessie. The long hallways and various nooks and corners hid me well enough. She hardly looked left or right, having no reason to believe that someone might be following her."

"I was just getting ready to search the Duke's study."

"I will be a gentleman and accompany you. I cannot have my beautiful fiancée roaming around alone in this ghostly mansion. It will also give me a chance to take a look at the Duke's place of work. You can tell a lot about a man from his personal space."

She nodded and turned away. She busied herself looking for a candle to take along.

The ensuing silence reminded her again of the Earl's presence in her room. She glanced at the bed and reddened.

She wanted to speak, to break the mounting tension but was afraid her voice would tremble and betray her.

The Earl smiled watching her flustered demeanour. He waited until she had lit the candle and moved towards the exit before grabbing her arm and halting her.

Emma's fingers tightened around the candle. She peeked at his face and his expression set her heart racing.

He stared at her exquisite face glowing in the firelight. He drank in her features, his fingers itching to take the pins out of her hair.

"If I don't kiss you now . . . it would be tragic," he said huskily.

"Angels would weep," she replied, nodding fervently.

He smiled briefly before stooping down and giving her a hard, quick kiss. He let her go immediately and said, "For luck. After all, we venture into the lion's den tonight."

"Don't be absurd," replied Emma, her heart still thundering in her chest.

She was secretly relieved to have the Earl with her. She had not been looking forward to sneaking into the Duke's study, but with him by her side it felt more like an adventure than an odious task. She was suddenly excited and peeked out of her room with enthusiasm.

Seeing that the coast was clear, she gestured to the Earl to follow.

They tiptoed their way towards the stairs, cupping the candle to dim the glow. Emma knew which bits of wood creaked and silently indicated the same to him.

They reached the bottom step and turned into a hallway. She led the way to the Duke's study, and after making sure that no light showed under the crack in the door, they cautiously entered the room.

She went straight towards a tray of letters left at the edge of a large mahogany desk. Those were the ones that the Duke would have written today. Pickering would post them in the morning.

She carefully set the candle on the table, and taking out a paper knife she got to work. She heated the steel blade and slipped it under the seal of the first letter.

The pile of letters was not large, and it would take them at most an hour to finish the task. They scanned and re-sealed the letters as quickly as they could.

They finally found one addressed to a man named Nutters, who it seemed was a private investigator in London. It mentioned the gardener, although briefly. Most of the letter was comprised of requesting information about an investigation the Duke had already engaged the man for. The Duke never said clearly what the matter was. It was all very vague, but his words in the end were ominous.

"What does Uncle mean by this bit?" Emma asked, pointing to a section in the letter.

The Earl silently read the contents:

'I need to know if I have to take any drastic action regarding the issue. The situation is steadily becoming worse, and it is now hard to sift the truth from lies. I have to protect my family and would appreciate it if you could speed up your investigations. Hire as many men as you need. You shall be compensated. I am getting desperate, and all my hopes now rest on your findings'

He pursed his lips thoughtfully, "I have no clue what he means. It sounds as if the he is in some sort of trouble. He doesn't specify anything, so it seems he is already suspicious of the letter falling into the wrong hands. I wonder who he suspects would dare to go through his mail. He mentions the gardener only briefly. He hasn't even finished that sentence before he starts talking about this other problem. I think this Nutters chap will write to the Duke asking him to explain more fully about the gardener, and that, unfortunately, means another night of searching through his letters."

"Poor uncle, I wonder what is worrying him."

"A Duke is bound to have a dozen problems. I don't think we should worry ourselves about anything other than our own concerns. After all, he seems to have hired a professional to sort it out for him. We cannot do anything more."

"I suppose," said Emma doubtfully.

"Come, it's time for bed."

Seeing her horrified face, he laughed. "I meant, you go to your bed, and I shall go to mine. Don't worry, your virtue is safe . . . at least for the moment," he added wickedly.

He stole a quick kiss before letting her escape.

Emma turned away and made her way back to her room. The Earl left for the servants' staircase hidden in the hallway. Emma blew out the candle and slipped into bed. She felt a pang of pity for the Earl, who would be sleeping on a hard, flea infested mattress. She put her feet on the hot bricks and reviewed the night in her mind.

The letter the Duke had written worried her. He had sounded unlike himself, pleading for information from the unknown Nutters. Emma would have never guessed anything was bothering the Duke. He seemed so calm and in control. No matter how many times she repeated the words from the letter in her head, she could not guess what the Duke meant. She sighed and closed her eyes.

Her last thought was not of the Duke, or even Mrs Barker and her antics, but the Earl's face leaning in close to kiss her.

❖ ❖ ❖

Emma woke the next morning with a pounding headache. She went to the breakfast room dreading the thought of listening to Mrs Barker and her daughter Prudence's shrill tones. She clutched her sore head and prayed they were still in bed but was disappointed . . . .

Mrs Barker sat sipping tea and having a whispered conversation with Lady Babbage. Prudence and Catherine sat silently eating eggs on toast.

Prudence was not a morning person, and she would thankfully not utter a sound until she had consumed her chocolate and three cups of tea.

Emma fetched herself a slice of dry toast and a cup of coffee before joining them.

The Duchess was still in bed as she never came down for breakfast. She had explained to Emma that spirits were most active at night, and she could not afford to sleep when there was so much to be learned from them. The Duke would have already breakfasted and would be in his study.

Catherine surreptitiously glanced at Lady Babbage and then nodded a greeting to Emma. Emma understood the brief look; she did not need words to interpret what Catherine was trying to convey.

It was odd to see two such different personalities involved so deeply in conversation. They refrained from saying anything aloud, since Prudence sat a few feet away. They finished their breakfast in silence, which was finally broken by Prudence.

"What shall we do today? I do not feel like riding down to the village. It looks as if it is going to rain."

"A stroll in the garden?" suggested Catherine.

"Fine," Prudence replied grudgingly.

Her tone suggesting that she would rather be paying calls in London than be cooped up in the country.

Emma forced herself to calm down. There was no point in getting angry with Prudence. Even if she said anything, it would likely sail over her head.

They set out for their walk, and Lady Babbage trailed behind with her sewing basket. Emma soon left the party behind and made her way to the old gardener mucking about in the vegetable patch.

"Nice day."

The Earl grinned and said, "It looks like it is going to rain."

"Yes, but once it does rain, the roses will moisten and the scent of them will be divine," replied Emma.

"A girl after my own heart, who appreciates the scent of wet earth and drenched flowers."

"What are you planting?"

"This right here, miss, is the herb patch. I am going to plant some mint and rosemary."

"You will be a handy husband. We can let the head gardener go and let you take care of the grounds. See, I am already thinking like a wife and economizing."

"I don't think I could look at another leaf without shuddering in future. Studying a text is rather different from the actual work involved. I am going to double my gardener's wage once I am home. By God, the man deserves it." He paused to put away his spade, "Do you think you can walk to the apple orchard and meet me where we met last time?"

"I am not sure," said Emma hesitatingly, glancing back. Prudence and Catherine were fast approaching.

"Try," he coaxed.

"Oh, alright, you go on ahead, I will meet you in a moment."

Emma waited for the Earl to hobble away before turning to greet her cousin and Prudence.

"We are going back inside. I think I felt a drop," said Prudence, staring up at the grey sky.

Emma flicked a glance towards the orchard. "I have a mind to pick some apples. Cat, are you going to stay?"

Catherine shook her head. "I think you should come back with us, Emma. You know Father doesn't like us walking alone."

Emma scowled. "Oh, what can happen to me in broad daylight? These are his grounds, after all. I shall be perfectly safe."

Catherine stood uncertainly until a great big drop on her nose decided her. "Hurry, I don't want you to get wet and catch your death."

"I won't be a minute, you go on. You will see me before you reach the house."

Catherine nodded and taking Prudence's arm started walking back to the house. Emma noticed Lady Babbage doing the same, and with a sigh of relief quickly made her way towards the orchard.

The Earl stood waiting on the outskirts. The rain started falling in earnest, and she was about to start running towards the apple trees, when through the sheet of rain, she noticed the Duke standing and watching her approach the gardener.

The Earl had noticed the Duke as well. She stood torn for a moment, and then changed her direction, moving towards the rose garden instead. She pretended not to see the Duke. She took that route to wind her way back towards the mansion.

The Earl, meanwhile, disappeared into the orchard. "That Duke," he moaned aloud, "will be the death of me."

Chapter 9

Catherine watched Emma race by her soaked to the bone. She shook her head in exasperation. She stopped a passing maid and asked her to bring a pot of tea to Emma's room.

Her cousin was a nightmare to deal with when she had the slightest sniffle.

She made her way to her father's study. Her father always kept some brandy on hand for medicinal purposes. A shot of brandy in Emma's tea would do her the world of good.

The Duke's study was open, and Catherine paused. She could hear voices inside, and wondered if she should disturb the Duke. He often had visitors who came to him with confidential problems. And, being the Duke, he was meant to help and solve those issues.

She turned to leave when Mrs Barker's voice arrested her.

Mrs Barker was speaking to the Duke in urgent tones.

Catherine bit her lip, torn between going in and rescuing her father or listening to what was being said. A year ago she would have walked away, but recently parts of her personality she never knew existed were coming out.

Instead of leaving or even interrupting the conversation, she felt a thrill go through her as she deliberately inched forward to hear them talk. She hoped Mrs Barker was being put in her place, and she wanted to catch every word if that were the case.

She heard Mrs Barker speak, "You know what I am offering. You are an intelligent man. You can't expect me to spell it out."

A brief silence indicated that the Duke had refused to answer.

Mrs Barker spoke again, and this time her tone was pleading, "We both are unhappy . . . and I cannot forget . . . "

Catherine strained her ears in frustration. Mrs Barker had started whispering, and she could no longer hear her words.

The Duke finally spoke loudly and clearly, "I have work to do, and I do not want to discuss this any further. Please do not embarrass either of us, Mrs Barker. Catherine, you may come in."

Catherine jumped guiltily. She entered the study and found a red-faced Mrs Barker, while the Duke looked angry. She realised he had seen her reflection in the Venetian mirror hanging over the fireplace.

In her eagerness to be naughty, for once, she had forgotten about that. She silently cursed and glanced apologetically at her father.

He smiled slightly in response and asked, "You wanted something?"

"Some brandy for Emma. She got caught in the rain, and I don't want her to fall ill."

The Duke opened the drawer in his desk and handed her a flask. His eyes twinkled, and Catherine blushed at being caught doing something as childish as eavesdropping. She quickly snatched the bottle and left.

❖ ❖ ❖

The mood in the house changed considerably with the onset of rain. The Duchess looked even more distracted than usual. She kept muttering to herself and forgot to pour the tea, in spite of being prompted by Catherine five times.

Prudence was disgusted to be hidden away in the country, bemoaning the fact that the season was over. She had exhausted the topic of how many men had asked her to marry them and how she had turned each one of them down. She had nothing more to offer.

Emma was worried about being caught walking alone once again by the Duke and him possibly realising that her goal had been to meet the gardener. Lady Babbage gave her a sympathetic look but did not ask her to confide again. Emma was grateful and sat by the old lady, finding her silence and the rhythmic click of needles soothing.

She kept waiting for the Duke to call her into his study and demand an explanation. But the entire evening and dinner went by, and the Duke behaved as though nothing was out of place. He did seem more thoughtful, and now that Emma knew to look for signs, she noticed the tired lines around his mouth. She felt slightly guilty for adding to his troubles.

Mrs Barker had resumed flirting with the Duke the moment he had stepped into the dining room. Mr Barker seemed to have gone back to enjoying his meals and was unaware of the mounting tension in the air.

The Duke looked grimmer and grimmer as the meal progressed, while Catherine was getting distressed and embarrassed. Lady Babbage's attempts to steer the conversation to neutral avenues was getting more frequent and desperate.

Mrs Barker showed her considerable skill by turning the discussion of cabbage soup into an invitation for the Duke to join her in bed.

Emma was shocked and joined Catherine in her mortification. She wondered how long it would be before the Duke lost his patience.

Yet no one spoke a word of admonishment the entire night. Everyone felt it was not their place to say something. The only person who had that right was Mr Barker, who seemed immune to his wife's blatant flirtation with another man.

Emma thought Mr Barker was secretly hoping that the Duke would take his wife off his hands.

Everyone retired to their rooms feeling dissatisfied and troubled.

Emma once again got ready to steal into the Duke's study. She was disappointed that the Earl didn't join her. She repeated the process of the night before and didn't find a single letter mentioning the gardener. Surprised, she turned in for the night. She knew the Duke had not forgotten. She would have to continue her nightly investigations.

❖ ❖ ❖

"I have a wonderful plan."

Emma groaned. In spite of the Duke's suspicions, she had still sought the Earl out and once again stood by a flower bed. Catherine and Prudence were seated on a stone bench not far away. This gave her considerable more time with the Earl.

"I do not like your plans," Emma objected.

"It's just a tweak in the already existing plan," the Earl coaxed.

"What is it?" she asked worriedly

"You are going to romance the gardener."

"Have your wits been addled? Have you inhaled the fumes of some odd fertilizer that is turning your brain into flea-mint?"

"Think about it, Em, if the Duke sees you spending a lot of time with an old man like me, then he may want to speed up this entire marriage issue."

"He would never believe that I am having an affair with a

commoner old enough to be my father."

"A lot of women like older men, and how is he to know what your taste runs to? It would make him sit up and take another look at this entire delaying the wedding situation. I mean, if you are falling all over yourself for an ancient gap-toothed man, then a year is a long time for you to fall for any sort and slip up."

"He would never believe it. It is too absurd."

"He is already suspicious. We have been acting like we have been caught doing something naughty every time he has met us, and that has already laid down the groundwork. All you have to do is meet me more blatantly and talk about me a lot more. Throw in how wonderful I am and how much I know of leaves and roots during dinner or something."

"I cannot do that! No one would believe it, and I can't have them thinking I am some sort of blatant hussy!"

The Earl chuckled, "Fine, do not mention me, but do not run away either the next time the Duke catches us." He caught her hand and added slyly, "It is not as if you are trying to keep away from me in any case."

Emma had no reply to that, so with a short nod, she reluctantly agreed. Then she changed the subject and told him about her investigations and Mrs Barkers behaviour.

The Earl was thoughtful. "I am not surprised that some woman is throwing herself at him. He is, after all, a Duke, and it is well known that his wife is mad. As far as I am aware he has no mistress, and Mrs Barker may be looking to fill that role. Mr Barker sounds like he doesn't really care what she does. So stop worrying. The Duke is old enough to choose his own diversions. As for him having still not written to your father or to me . . . it is odd."

"I think he will write today. Will you be able to get away?"

"I will do my best to try and meet you in your rooms tonight."

Catherine called out that moment to say they were returning indoors.

Emma quickly brushed off her muddy skirt as best as she could and made her way towards the manor. At the entrance, she encountered the Duke, who eyed the dirt on her skirt with pursed lips.

Whether she wanted to or not, the Duke, it seemed, was drawing the exact conclusions the Earl wanted him to draw. Emma walked away wanting to half laugh and half cry.

Chapter 10

The Earl met her that night, and Emma greeted him in relief. Her aunt's vivid imagination was hard to laugh off when the manor was plunged in darkness and every tiny sound amplified. She had been afraid of running into the Duchess' spirit friends.

They went about the business quickly, the Earl too impatient to even steal a kiss.

Emma pounced on the first letter that lay on the table. It was addressed to her father. She quickly took it off the tray and unsealed it. Sure enough, it requested details of the head gardener that Lord Hamilton had recommended.

Emma pocketed it, intending to reply herself, and then ask the Earl's valet to send it to London. It would then be posted back to the Duke so that it had the London mark on the envelope. It would delay the letter, but that could be blamed on the post.

Next they found another envelope marked to Lord Hamilton. They left that alone, as it would reach the Earl's London home and then be forwarded to his valet. The Earl could reply to that when it reached him. There was nothing else of significance, and they retired to their respective rooms, with Emma only receiving a half-hearted kiss.

The Earl was preoccupied with wondering how he could speed up the entire plan. The weeks seemed to stretch before him, and he wanted to get this entire thing over with as soon as possible. He had not had a single night's good rest. He was getting impatient, and it hadn't even been a week yet.

❖ ❖ ❖

The next day Emma woke up feeling miserable. She wanted to speak to the Earl but was in no mood to search the grounds for him.

Therefore, she cornered Pickering and inquired as to the whereabouts of the head gardener.

Pickering paused briefly, an expression of surprise almost crossing his face, before he calmly replied that the man in question was in the Night Garden. Emma thanked him and quickly set off in that direction. She found the Earl seated on the edge of a marble fountain.

"Good evening, I did not expect to see you until tonight. Has something happened?" the Earl asked.

"Yes, no, I mean nothing has happened as such, but something has been worrying me, and I wanted to talk to you."

He patted the seat next to himself and Emma sat down.

"Does it not bother you to be going through the Duke's papers? I find it deceitful and do not like it at all."

The Earl did not smile but instead said reflectively, "It is not honourable, but we never go through any of the letters addressed to his estate manager, close family friends, or even the Duchess' physician. You know most of the people that the Duke corresponds with, and you make sure to read only the first few lines of any letter written to anyone you have not previously heard of."

The Earl paused to pull out a package wrapped in brown paper. He undid the strings and offered it to Emma.

She found the paper full of berries. She chose one carefully before saying, "I do try, but something like that letter to Nutters was so personal. I don't think it is right that we were privy to it. Reading letters written to my father is a different matter, since he has always allowed me to deal with such things."

"We mean no harm and our intentions are, if not good, then only mischievous. Don't worry about it so much. I will meet you tonight as usual, and we will try to be more careful and not read more than necessary. He may still write to Nutters, and we need to make sure that letter does not reach its destination."

"I wish . . ."

"What is it?"

"I wish I could spend more time with you. Our stolen moments together do not feel like enough."

He glanced at her wistful face and felt an answering pang of longing. "Why don't you wear an old frock tomorrow, one you don't mind getting dirty, and carry a pair of garden gloves? Ask Lady

Babbage for permission and join me in the garden. Tell her you want to learn something about growing flowers since you intend to have a patch of your own once you are married."

"We can spend the day together, and if Lady Babbage wants, she can sit on a bench and keep watch over me. The Duke cannot complain," said Emma delighted.

"So I take it that you will join me?"

"Yes, I will," she promised, considerably cheered.

❖ ❖ ❖

Mrs Barker was silent that evening. She snapped at Lady Babbage more than once, and Prudence looked bored.

Catherine suggested a game of cards to improve tempers, and the women quickly agreed. No one was in a mood to converse, and the competitive game improved their spirits somewhat.

The Duchess won every round, which came as no surprise. The woman had the devil's own luck in cards. Her grace declared it was her dear departed father who always aided her.

Emma, having lost all her pennies, silently agreed that her aunt's good luck was uncanny, unless she cheated, but that thought was laughable in itself. The Duchess could not possibly know how to cheat at cards, nor did she have the patience or the presence of mind to use sleight of hand.

They all retired to bed early that evening. Things were getting dull in the house.

Emma met the Earl that night feeling more secure about their nightly adventures. She assumed everything would go as usual. She was mistaken. Things started to go wrong the minute the Earl met her.

"I think Pickering is suspicious. He asked me where I disappear to at night. It seems he has seen me slip out of bed more than once. He could have followed me before, but I am not sure."

"How can you be sure that he hasn't followed you again?"

"I slipped a sedative into his cup this evening. It is a perk of being a gardener and knowing my plants. He will sleep like a log the entire night, but I cannot keep dosing him, or he will get suspicious."

"I hope we find a letter written to Nutters regarding your status. I am getting weary of this nightly prowling."

"I agree, we cannot keep doing this. We are sure to be discovered sooner than later."

Emma picked up the candle and made her way out into the hallway.

They had walked down the main staircase and turned the corner towards the Duke's study when they heard the unmistakable sound of a floorboard creak.

"It came from the stairs," whispered Emma in fright.

The Earl held his finger to his lips and peered around the corner to look at the staircase.

Emma joined him and stifled a gasp.

A ghostly figure in black was slowly descending the stairs. A candle held aloft in one hand was throwing flickering shadows on the face. The figure was tall and straight, while the skin looked unnaturally pale.

Emma dug her nails into the Earl's arm. He grasped her hand and held it.

They watched transfixed as the vision moved slowly down the steps. The closer it moved, the more aware Emma became of the fact that she knew that face. The carriage was different, yet the features looked remarkably familiar.

The figure stopped on the bottom step, and Emma suddenly knew whom she looked at.

The Earl pulled her quickly towards the study. They hid inside and blew out the candle. After a moment, they heard footsteps approaching the door. The person paused outside briefly and then moved on. Emma waited for a few moments before sagging against the Earl.

She clutched his shirt sleeve and said, "That was Lady Babbage. I barely recognised her. I always have this notion of her bending over a piece of cloth or wool. She seemed taller, and I have never seen that expression on her face before."

"What do you suppose she was doing roaming around so late at night? I had assumed it was the Duchess on her walks hunting down spirits."

Emma was surprised she hadn't thought of that as well. She was also a trifle embarrassed that her first thought instead had been that the woman was a ghost.

"She may have been unable to sleep and went to fetch a book in the library."

"Except that she was fully dressed and looked as though she was going out," he replied.

"Perhaps she never changed, though I recall she wore a dull blue dress tonight . . . not black."

"Odd . . . Well, we can't go through the papers today as the candle is out. I don't think we will be able to find a tinder box in the dark. Besides, I am afraid Lady Babbage may catch us. We can't afford to take that risk. I suggest we retire for the night and pray the Duke has not written to Nutters yet."

"With the way my luck has gone tonight, I wouldn't be surprised if he has. Oh, well, we can't do more. Goodnight, Richard."

The Earl, instead of answering, pulled her close. It was a considerable time before Emma reached her room.

❖ ❖ ❖

Next morning, Catherine and Prudence left for the village accompanied by the Duchess. Mrs Barker said she felt a little under the weather and decided to stay home.

Meanwhile, Emma, garbed in a faded grey dress, sought out Lady Babbage, who agreed to accompany her, finding her request for learning more about plants perfectly acceptable.

Pickering informed her that the head gardener could be found in the Oriental Garden. That man, Emma mused, knew where every single soul was on the entire estate. He had barely given a thought before answering her.

Sure enough, the Earl was bending over some exotic plant, turning the earth with his fingers. An under-gardener who looked to be around thirty sat listening to whatever the Earl was saying.

They both glanced up as Emma approached. The Earl smiled in welcome, his blackened teeth causing her amusement.

She glanced at the man next to him and was shocked to see pure loathing on his face. Emma turned to see what he was looking at and found the source of his ire — Lady Babbage.

Lady Babbage had barely glanced at the two men and missed the look directed her way. She found a stone bench and pulling out her needles calmly prepared to work.

By the time Emma turned around, she found the under-gardener already walking away. The Earl sat staring after him.

"What do you think that was about?" Emma asked, pulling on her gloves.

"Who knows? Perhaps she offended him some time. The rich are often insensitive to the plight of lesser born. I am ashamed to admit that I, too, have been callous towards servants at times. At the time, I was unaware of the hurt I was inflicting. Still, it is no excuse. We really must learn to be more sensitive. That young man is new here, and I think he was in a better position until some misfortune robbed him of his luck. He has not had time to grow the thick skin needed to live the life of a servant."

"Don't be sad . . . Come tell me what to do? I might as well learn something while I am here."

Emma spent some time learning how to weed. While she was pulling out the unwanted roots, she asked, "Whom do you love the most in your family?"

"You know I lost my parents at a young age?"

At Emma's nod, he continued. "I was eighteen at the time and my sister only twelve. I suppose out of those alive she is the one person I treasure most."

"She is married to a marquis now, isn't she?"

"Yes, very happily married. They are expecting a baby."

"How wonderful. I can't wait to meet her, I suppose she was in the country due to her condition, which is why I missed meeting her during my season in London."

"Another two months and we will have a new admission in our family. I, of course, intend to make sure we have our own first born before she manages to conceive her next child."

"It is not a race, My Lord," said Emma blushing.

"Oh, but it is, especially since I intend to have at least ten before I am too old."

"Ten children!" said Emma laughing. "Surely you jest."

The Earl's eyes warmed as he watched her face light up.

"I have been trying to ask you something."

Emma sobered, hearing the strain in the Earl's voice.

"I tried a few times but something always diverted us."

"What is it?" asked Emma, her heart beating fast. Something in his tone alerted her as to his intent.

"Emma, what are you doing here?"

Emma leaped up, brushing her hands on her skirt, forgetting she was wearing muddy gloves. Mrs Barker stood with the Duke staring at her in shock.

Chapter 11

Emma addressed the Duke, "I was learning how to weed. I intend to have my own garden, and this seemed the best way to learn."

"I thought I told you not to wander out alone."

A flash of anger crossed Emma's face before it was quickly concealed. She hated the way the Duke tried to run everyone's life, never allowing anyone, not even his own daughter, to walk unaccompanied in her own home.

"I am not alone. Lady Babbage is sitting right there, and I had asked her permission," she said defensively.

The Duke looked down at her face and rightly guessed her thoughts. He let out a tired sigh and said, "Forgive me, I did not notice her."

Emma gave a short nod.

The Duke waited for a moment before walking away with Mrs Barker clinging to his arm.

"That Duke . . . " muttered the Earl, prudently keeping the rest of his thoughts to himself.

Their pleasant moment together was ruined. She spent the next hour staying silent while he softly pointed out some plant or the other.

He could see she was not attending, and he finally suggested that she should go back indoors. The day was becoming chilly, and she was not warmly dressed.

Lady Babbage took Emma's arm and they started walking back.

"That gardener is not what he seems," she said idly.

Emma tripped, and after steadying herself said, "Whatever do you mean?"

"He is younger than he is pretending to be, isn't he?"

Emma turned to face her in shock.

"I noticed his face was not lined. He had more agility than a man of his age should have had. Is he someone you love? Someone you do not want the Earl to know about?"

"No! It's nothing like that."

"I was young once and know what it is to love without a care for status and riches. The Earl is a rich man and an excellent match. I perfectly understand your feelings, my dear. You can confide in me, you know."

"I don't know what you mean. I would never do that to a man I was betrothed to. I am not having an affair, and I didn't notice anything odd about the gardener."

A flash of irritation crossed Lady Babbage's face, and she tightened her grip on Emma's arm. It took her a moment to compose herself and say soothingly, "I apologise, I think of you as I think of Catherine. Even if I am not your chaperone, you have, after all, grown up in this household. Your parents may not have appointed me your guardian, but the Duke surely intends for me to care for you just as I do for his own daughter. I have seen you every summer from the time you were born. I think I have earned the right to caution you. I did not mean to overstep my bounds."

Emma refused to speak. They were rapidly approaching the house, and she quickened her steps.

Lady Babbage had no trouble keeping up. She continued speaking, "I have learnt to observe people around me and understand them. I see more than people think I do, and I know that man is a fraud. You, my dear, are still young and are as yet unaware of the world. I would request you to be careful."

"I thank you for your concern, but I assure you, I am doing nothing that would shame the Earl in any way," Emma replied nervously and then hurriedly changed the topic. "Did you ask Catherine to study human nature like you do?"

"I am often overlooked, and Catherine is a lot like me," said Lady Babbage, her face softening as she spoke. "That girl is intelligent and a fast learner. I did nudge her in the right direction. People like us prefer to watch rather than be watched."

Emma eyed her sceptically.

Lady Babbage spoke more forcefully. "We prefer such an existence, and I know for a fact that it is far more fruitful and peaceful than being the centre of attention."

Emma, who had spent an entire season in London trying to get noticed and feeling terrible at being snubbed, had a difficult time grasping Lady Babbage's meaning. She could not imagine how it was more wonderful to be a wallflower than the belle of the ball.

"I have forgotten my needles," Lady Babbage said, interrupting her thoughts, "you do not need to accompany me back. I am allowed to walk about alone. Go back to the house, I will see you at dinner."

She watched Lady Babbage return the way they had come. She had never realised the depths that someone she had known all her life hid from the world. The woman was more complex than she had given her credit for.

Yet, in spite of her protestations of being content, Emma had heard the underlying tone of bitterness lacing her words.

❖ ❖ ❖

"Young man, have you seen my sewing basket?"

"It must be on the stone bench." The Earl glanced up to see a satisfied smile on the Lady Babbage's face. He realised his mistake. He continued uneasily, "But you jest, My Lady, I have not been a young man for years."

"Could you fetch the basket for me?" Lady Babbage asked, instead of answering him.

The Earl was annoyed. The woman could walk the few steps herself.

"My hands are filthy, My Lady."

"I don't mind. I am tired of walking."

The Earl walked the few steps and carefully picked up the basket with the tips of his fingers and handed it to her.

He had often bid his valet fetch him a glass of brandy when he could have reached the drink himself by stretching out his hand. He had never before realised how annoying his request would have been to his servant.

"So are you a second son or perhaps one of her tutors?"

"Pardon, madam?"

"An old man would not have gotten up so fluidly after kneeling for hours on the ground."

"I am simply blessed with good bones. Why, my father . . ."

"I do not have time to play games. I know you are courting Emma, and you are obviously not rich enough or of her status;

hence, this charade to stay close to her."

He stared at her, carefully masking his expression. There was something cruel in her face as she spoke.

"I should inform the Duke, but I will not."

"That is very kind of you, but I assure you that you are mistaken."

"I am not mistaken, and I am not kind. I think having you under my thumb will work well to my advantage. When the time comes, I will tell you what I want you to do for me."

"You will resort to blackmail? It will not work on me."

Lady Babbage raised an eyebrow. "You need to think of Emma and her reputation. If I let slip what I suspect . . . she will be a ruined."

"You have known her since she was a babe. You would never hurt her."

"You do not know me or my relationship with the girl. She has ignored me and my advice every summer. Unlike Catherine, she never even pretended to like me. I couldn't care less about her."

The Earl frowned. "You can tell the Duke if you like, but I don't think he will find anything unseemly. You will make a fool of yourself."

Lady Babbage smiled and said, "So you continue to lie to me? You will sing a different tune soon enough."

She received a blank submissive look of a good servant for her efforts in return. She stood for a moment looking at him uncertainly, then shook her head and walked away.

❖ ❖ ❖

That night, instead of finding the Earl hiding under her bed, Emma found a note:

Pickering did not take his nightly ale and I could not dose him. DO NOT venture out alone to the Duke's study. I will tell you more when I see you.

Yours

Richard

"Yours Richard," Emma grumbled. Why had he not written love?

She crumpled the note and threw it into the fire. She watched it burn and wondered why he didn't want her to investigate on her own. He could have written another line explaining.

She wanted to disobey him and search the study, but the vision of Lady Babbage with the candle swam before her eyes.

She admitted to herself that she was not brave enough to venture out alone. Taking the coward's way out, Emma decided to stay in her room that night.

❖ ❖ ❖

The next morning Emma sat at the table poking holes into her boiled eggs. The Duchess had woken early and joined them for a change.

Mrs Barker enthusiastically shook salt all over her plate. "Your Grace, I compliment you on how well this household is run. It is so hard to find good servants these days. Though, I admit, I have never had any trouble dealing with them personally. My mother taught me the art of running a smooth household. But lately I have heard of servants putting on airs and graces, trying to act well above their station."

The Duchess looked up in surprise. "My housekeeper deals with them. She is highly efficient. I leave everything in her capable hands."

"I agree, people of our class should stay well away from dealing with their kind. They can be so temperamental. One must not get too familiar with them," Mrs Barker said, looking at Emma.

Emma fumed. She considered her maid Bessie to be a thousand times more refined than Mrs Barker, irrespective of her status in society.

The Duke looked concerned at the direction the conversation had taken. He spoke now, "Emma, can I request your presence in my study after you have eaten?"

"Yes, uncle," she replied, her heart hammering.

This was it. Either the Duke had discovered the truth, or he wanted to scold her for chatting with the gardener like a commoner. Neither option soothed her fears.

Chapter 12

"Enter," the Duke called out.

"You wanted to speak to me?"

The Duke looked up from his desk and set aside his pen. "Ah, yes, Emma. Please sit. I don't like you hovering over me like that. Would you care for some tea?"

"No, thank you, I had plenty during breakfast."

"Are you happy here, Emmy?"

She felt tears prick her eyes at hearing her childhood name spoken after so many years. Her parents still called her Emmy, but the Duke had long given it up.

"I have always been happy here, uncle."

"I hope you still consider this as your home and know that you can confide in me if anything troubles you."

Emma nodded, not wanting to speak the lie.

He waited for her to continue, and at length when she did not, he said, "I am concerned about you spending so much time with the gardener. Do not misunderstand me. I have nothing against servants. I value Pickering above a number of lords and ladies. I often take his advice, and he mentioned how you have been seeking out the gardener again and again. I know your intentions are honourable and I trust you, but servants have an unfortunate habit of gossiping, and your preference has been noted and commented upon. Even Mrs Barker hinted at something unsavoury regarding your conduct this morning."

He held up his hand when Emma would have spoken, "Hear me out. I know she is a gossipy, vulgar woman, and you should normally ignore all she says. But in this instance such talk could ruin your future prospects. Since you are so newly engaged, the Earl may not find such conduct agreeable in a wife."

"I understand, uncle, but I assure you, the Earl would have nothing to be embarrassed about. I have behaved like a lady, and it is not fair to say I cannot learn the nuances of planting flowers because someone like her objects."

"You may learn it after you are wed," the Duke snapped and then taking a deep breath continued more gently, "I know why you are here after such a short courtship. I guessed the Earl was not happy with the delay in the wedding plans. I did it for you so that you may not regret marrying the man years later. I made the mistake of marrying the current Duchess too soon. We had known each other for only four months. The constrictions of society never allowed us enough time together to get to know each other properly. I still regret that decision. I did not want the same to happen to you."

Emma's heart clenched in pain. "I am sorry, uncle, I confess I had been angry with you, and I thank you for the explanation. I appreciate your concern and understand your reasons better now. I do feel that you are right in your thinking, but you don't know the Earl. I have spent a lot of time with him going on rides and picnics. One may spend years living with someone without understanding them. At the same time, you can rightly judge a man within five minutes of meeting him. Marriage is a risk, uncle, and I believe I know the Earl well enough to take that risk. I am so afraid he will be snatched away from me that I'd rather not wait."

The Duke leaned back in his chair, his face thoughtful. "I did not want to tell you as it was to be a surprise. When I saw you gardening with that man with not a care for propriety, I realised that parting from your betrothed so soon was making you unhappy, and you were seeking a diversion. With Mrs Barker making such vicious comments about how she found you this morning, the situation is direr. She will let the word out, and I do not want the Earl, if he is a good man, to judge you wrongly. So I am pleased that I have already written to the Earl and invited him to visit us here. He can see for himself what the source of gossip is like. I can meet the man you have chosen, and if I find him worthy of you, then you have my blessings to marry when you choose."

Emma's smile had grown bigger and bigger as her uncle spoke, and now she leapt from her chair and rushed to hug him like she used to as a child.

"Thank you! Thank you! You are the nicest, kindest, most

wonderful uncle in the whole wide world!"

The Duke laughed and gently pushed her away.

"Now go, I know you are dying to tell your cousin the latest news. I hope he arrives soon enough for your sake."

Laughing, Emma ran out and went not to look for Catherine, but once again, the head gardener.

She sneaked out the back, taking care to avoid Pickering or anyone who could be watching. She knew the Duke would not expect her to go looking for the gardener, not after the talk they had just had, but this was too exciting for her to keep to herself.

She found him smoking a pipe in the apple orchard.

"I have news," she panted.

"I need to talk to you," he said at the same time.

Because she was still catching her breath, the Earl decided to go first.

"Lady Babbage tried to blackmail me."

Emma took one look at his face and sat right where she stood. She patted the grass next to her, and the Earl joined her.

"She came to me yesterday after dropping you back to the house," the Earl said.

"To fetch her work basket?"

"That was just an excuse. She has guessed that I am younger than I look, and she knows something is going on between us, though she is still in the dark as to my identity. She wants me to do something for her, and if I don't, she has threatened to tell the Duke or the Earl."

"But you must be mistaken. Why would she do something like this? She lives in comfort, and what could she possibly gain? She did hint her misgivings to me, but she said it was out of concern. It truly did not sound as if she had some nefarious plan."

"She wanted you to talk, and once you did, she would blackmail you as well. I hope you did not confide in her."

He continued after her reassurance that she had kept it all to herself. "She will approach me when she has a job for me to do. She said so clearly, and if I do not comply, then she promised to make me suffer, even if it means ruining your name. She dislikes you, she said, for you have never heeded her advice and always neglected her . . . I do hope she writes to the Earl instead of going to the Duke. Imagine me receiving my own complaint. My reply would be colourful enough to set her right for good."

"It is true, I never liked her, but I never hated her or deliberately snubbed her. I was young, bound to break some rules and disregard her presence, but resorting to blackmail seems a bit extreme. She may have been bluffing . . . I cannot imagine her being capable of such things. She is a sweet old boring lady. She was trying to scare you into leaving me alone."

"Trust me, and stay away from her. That sweet old lady has tiny horns protruding from her head. I am sure she hides them in that nest of dry brown hair. That woman has her own agenda. I don't know what it is yet, but I intend to ferret it out. Meanwhile, I want you to stay in your room and no more searching the Duke's study. If she catches us, then we would have a lot more to worry about than the Duke discovering my identity. Searching through his personal belongings is a far more serious matter."

"That is why you left the note for me last night. Well, what I have to tell you would throw water on Lady Babbage's plans. Put out that smelly pipe first. My poor nose cannot take it anymore."

The Earl took a long drag, and then reluctantly put it away. Emma then proceeded to recount the morning events.

"I am not sure if this is good news," he replied.

"Whatever do you mean? You can give up this entire charade and present yourself to the Duke. You still get to live in the same house but this time with all the comforts. I can meet you more frequently and openly. How is that not a good thing?"

"The Duke has had a hard marriage. He may think I am a fine young man, but there is no guarantee he will admit it. He will think of something else to delay the wedding. His main concern is your behaviour, which he feels needs to be curtailed. You do not seem to listen to his authority, so he hopes my presence will curb your wild ways and keep you passive. He will then attempt to convince me to wait a little longer, and I will have no decent counterargument. My instinct tells me that we are right for each other, but that is not going to go down well with a practical man."

"So what do you suggest?"

"I want to continue this charade. The main reason being, I have spent almost a week sweating and labouring in this very field. I do not want that to go waste and declare defeat. My wager still stands, and I aim to see this thing through."

"Oh, forget this silly game. I concede defeat, and you have won the wager. Now, please just come and stay as yourself. I will even admit to being compromised, and there will be no reason to stall the wedding after that."

"It is the principle of things. I have to win the wager fairly, not because my fiancée suddenly feels sorry that I have to sleep on a flea infested mattress. No, Em, I am sorry, but it is just a matter of another three weeks. I will see this entire thing through."

"That's all very well, but the Duke expects the Earl to arrive any moment now. He sent the letter a few days ago. Remember, we saw it. It would be rude not to answer his request for your presence. Besides, a fiancée would be clamouring to be with his betrothed. You can't weasel out of it using a business excuse."

The Earl was silent for a moment. At length, he brightened and said, "I know the perfect man for the job."

"Job?"

"Yes, it's brilliant. Another tweak in our plan."

"No"

"Yes"

"No!"

"Please, hear me out at least."

"Fine," she replied, crossing her arms.

"I can continue to be the head gardener, and someone else can take my place as the Earl. No one on the estate has met me before. They will never know!"

"They will meet you on the wedding day. Then what?"

"They will hardly stop the wedding over a tiny bit of play acting."

"Hardly tiny," she muttered and then said more loudly, "So now you mean to bring another actor into this entire façade? You will continue impersonating the gardener while someone else will impersonate you? This is giving me a headache! Is there anyone you can trust to such an extent?"

"Yes, Em. It's the perfect plan."

"Not your Valet, Richard. You cannot be thinking of that man! Why, he resembles a fat, overripe tomato!"

"No, I am not thinking of Burns. I am thinking of the honourable marquis's eldest son, Lord William Raikes."

"You are funning me. That man hasn't set foot in England, why . . . since he turned eighteen."

"He has recently returned to England as his father is ailing. I have been in touch with him over the years. We grew up together. His estate adjoins mine. You are mistaken in your belief that he has not visited England between his travels. He comes often, but he is a sort of recluse, keeping to himself a lot. He is a writer and has made quite a name for himself."

"I remember reading a book by 'W.S. Raikes'. It's in my father's study. I wonder if he is the same?"

"That's him alright, world renowned. He owes me a favour, and I think I will call on it now. No one will remember him from his youth as he has changed a lot since then. He is a gentleman with a similar background in education and aware of every part of my life. He is the only man who could convincingly pull it off."

"Is he a good actor?"

"I am not sure. He never played any roles in our school productions, since he loathed large crowds. But he is intelligent, so I am not worried."

"I don't like this. Your plan is getting more and more complex. We are bound to be caught."

"Isn't that what you want, to win the wager . . . or would you rather lose it?"

"Oh, what does it matter, the result is the same." She heard the church bell peal in the distance and sprang up.

"I have to go."

"Expect Raikes within a few days," the Earl shouted after her.

Chapter 13

"Oh, where is he?"

"Catherine, stop peeking out of the window. He may spot you. It will reflect badly on your cousin," Lady Babbage admonished.

How, Emma wondered, could a woman so entrenched in propriety blackmail anyone?

Lord William Raikes had dropped all his concerns to travel overnight in his well-sprung carriage as soon as he received his friend's missive.

As a result, a note had arrived in the morning to warn the Duke of the Earl of Hamilton's arrival. The ladies had been informed, and the news sent the feminine minds into a tizzy. They had immediately thrown themselves into a tumult of planning and readying the house for the guest. Now they sat demurely, pretending to have spent the hours sewing, instead of having mucked about in dust and dirt.

"Tell us what he looks like again, Em?" pleaded Prudence. The thought of a young man, even if engaged, had brought life back into her face. He was, after all, an Earl, and until he was married he was fair game for all.

Emma, who would have loved to discourse on the various attributes of the Earl in the past, did not know how to reply.

This Lord Raikes was bound to look different from Richard. He would surely not be as handsome, and how in the world was she to recognise him when he did arrive? She could mistakenly point to the valet, and then where would she be?

She remembered uneasily that she had spoken at length about the Earl's looks to Catherine. She hoped her cousin would put that down to a lover's exaggeration.

Prudence admitted she had seen the Earl twice. Both those times someone had pointed him out at a crowded ball, but she had never been able to secure an introduction. Fortunately, she had never seen him properly, the flitting bodies leaving an impression of a tall, handsome man. But his face was vague in her mind. Emma was thankful for that bit of luck at least.

The plan was developing even more holes. Soon she would not be able to keep up with all the lies.

"They are here!" Catherine squealed.

Emma tried to smile, and noticing Lady Babbage watching her, she forced herself to grin. The effect was disturbing.

"Is something the matter?" Catherine asked

"I am just really nervous," Emma replied. It was the truth.

"Come on, we must get ready for dinner. It is still another hour away, but I think we should all dress up for the occasion," Catherine said, taking hold of Emma's arm.

Prudence jumped up and rushed to the door before either of them could take a step, no doubt planning to outdo the cousins in their attempt to enthral the new arrival.

Emma grimaced and led the way out. She ascended the stairs and paused to look back at Catherine, who was no longer behind her. She looked over the rail and found her cousin staring at a man in the hallway. Their voices drifted up to her.

"Ah, I take it that you are the maid. Here is my hat . . . Take it, you silly thing. You must be new here. Now, where is the Duke's study?"

"Who are you?" Catherine snapped.

"I am the Earl of Hamilton, My Lord to you, and I forgive your insolence, since you were unaware of my identity. Now quickly, girl, where is the Duke's study?"

"But . . . but . . . " Catherine's stuttering was halted by the Duke's voice, and the man turned and walked away, leaving his hat in her outstretched hand.

Emma quickly ran to her room and contemplated barring her door. How had she got herself into such a fix?

"Emma?"

Better to get it over with. She opened the door.

"I just had the most curious encounter," Catherine said.

"Oh, with whom?" Emma asked innocently.

"I just met your Earl, but something was decidedly odd about him."

"What?"

"You told me that he had blonde hair."

"I may have exaggerated, it is more dark blonde."

"Yes, but — "

"Some would even think it brown. In some lights, it is decidedly dark brown."

"Yes, but this man . . . his hair . . . it was raven black!"

Emma gulped. Everyone knew the Earl was blonde. How could Richard have forgotten the colour of his best friend's hair? This was a complete disaster, and he had left her to deal with this entire mess alone.

"Maybe he has been out in the sun too long?"

"Emma, the sun darkens the skin and lightens the hair. You are not making any sense whatsoever."

Emma opened her closet and poked her head in. Hiding her face among the dresses, she finally spoke in a muffled voice, "Let me meet him at dinner, and then see if it were, in fact, the Earl that you spoke to. Perhaps you were mistaken." That was the best she could do for the moment.

"I was not mistaken. He told me his name clearly, and he was the one mistaken, for he took me for a common housemaid!"

She glanced at Catherine's face and silently cursed the newcomer. The moment he had stepped foot in the house he had already alienated one member of the family.

The Earl came up with the most idiotic plans. She would start suffering from nerves soon.

❖ ❖ ❖

Emma entered the dining room wearing a beautiful rose gown.

Catherine outshone her in a soft silver dress. She had taken his earlier offence to heart and wanted to show herself in all her aristocratic glory. He would not mistake her for a maid again.

Only one person was sitting on the sofa, and Emma could safely assume that this was the Earl's friend. She also noticed his jet black hair with a sinking heart.

"Emma!" The man rose from his seat and, unfortunately, looked directly at Catherine.

"It is good to see you again, My Lord. May I present, Lady Catherine Arden?" Emma quickly spoke.

Lord Raikes bowed formally to both of them.

"Emma has told me a lot about you, My Lord," Catherine said politely.

"I am sure all wonderful things that no man can live up to. I assure you, I am full of flaws."

"Oh, not everything she said was all . . . wonderful."

He was taken aback, unaware that Catherine was out for revenge for his earlier slight.

"Well, then," he paused, unable to continue.

Catherine's eyes gleamed, and Emma was delighted to see such a side in her normally demure cousin.

Prudence and Mrs Barker entered the room, followed by the Duchess.

Prudence had once again donned her teapot, and she immediately engaged the newcomer in a conversation. A bit of cold tea dribbled onto his excellent shoulders . . .

Emma watched the droplets splash onto Lord Raikes' blue evening coat and frowned. She caught his eye in silent appeal, wondering how she could warn him about the undeniable issue of his hair colouring.

He blinked uncomprehendingly.

She narrowed her eyes in irritation, and then recollecting the watching audience forced herself to smile. At least his eyes were blue, though darker than the Earl's, she consoled herself. She had to concede that Lord William Raikes was an exceptionally handsome man in a darkly, brooding sort of way. If only his hair had been lighter, the plan would have worked beautifully.

She raised her brow when he chanced to look her way again. She escaped to the balcony, hoping he would follow. After waiting for ten minutes, she strode back inside in annoyance to find him talking to her cousin again. From the heated flush on both their faces, it was clear the conversation was not going well.

She walked towards them and overheard Catherine say,

"But surely, My Lord, you must agree that women are capable of intelligence, if not superior, then at least on par with that of men?"

"I do not dispute that fact, Lady Arden. Yet saying that they should be allowed study at a university is ridiculous. You do not understand how many hours of work are required, nor do you know how the students live. Women should be protected from such an environment. You have your ladies institutes where women may study, and they are designed to bring out the best in you. All young ladies seem to be extraordinarily accomplished these days, and their talent in their own field cannot be matched by a man. Thereafter, you have to marry and bear children. It is a man's job to provide for the family and accordingly study further for his chosen occupation. What good would it do a woman?" Lord Raikes asked.

"You are simply afraid we would outshine you in your own field. That is why you choose to hold us back with brute strength rather than wit. Who is to say we are incapable of providing for our families? Governesses, teachers, maids and housekeepers all earn their keep. We cannot prove what we can or cannot do unless we are given a chance to compete with men on an equal footing."

"I agree they do a remarkable job, but can you imagine a woman in battle or venturing into dark caves for coal? Or perhaps arguing politics in her gentle voice? A female mind and body are created differently from a man, and we must focus on our strengths. A common university for both sexes would prove difficult to police. The women would not be safe, as it would be difficult to chaperone so many ladies and men present together for any length of time. As for men, why, the bevy of women would prove to be a distraction. We cannot have that interfering with the quality of education of our scholars. Even if a rare woman does excel and is admitted to a university, then what would happen to her thereafter? Who would marry her or offer her a post? What if she becomes pregnant? A job does not have the luxury to wait. It needs to be done there and then. No employer will wait nine months for his workers to return."

Catherine gasped. It was not done to speak of pregnancy so openly, not even amongst women. It was referred to as 'that delicate time' in hushed tones by close friends and between acquaintances never mentioned at all. Her embarrassment warred with her mounting anger as she glared at him. Her palms itched to slap his face, while her upbringing told her to introduce the topic of weather.

Emma knew Lord Raikes had travelled to various countries, and had no doubt forgotten how to behave like a gentleman. She had stayed silent, fascinated with the subject of the debate being conducted. She knew her cousin held some outlandish views, but she had never before heard her speak so passionately about her cause to a stranger.

She also recognised the look Catherine wore presently. The last time she had worn that expression, they had been fifteen years old, and Catherine had pulled a chunk of hair from the head of a village girl who had dared to mock Emma. One did not argue with the Duke's daughter and speak so candidly. No one else would have dared to say such things to Catherine.

She quickly intervened, "My Lord, I was looking for you." For a moment, she thought he would not recognise her.

He stared at her blankly and then said, "Emma?"

"It is a full moon tonight," she hinted.

"Yes, well . . . that is good. Bright, you know . . . for people walking home in the dark . . . err . . . keep them safe from footpads."

Emma waited for him to ask her to take a walk on the balcony. He did not.

She finally said, "Dinner will be served in a few moments. I hope you can wait?"

"Why, yes, I can." He turned to address Catherine, "When I was on an expedition in Egypt, I was accidently left behind in a pyramid chamber. I did not hear the party I had arrived with leave, since I was engrossed in examining a recently unearthed mummy. I had to go without food for two whole days. Thankfully I had enough water to survive a painful death through dehydration. Do not concern yourself. These few moments do not bother me."

Emma groaned. That man needed to stay in character. Her Earl would never forget his surroundings and calmly declare his unfortunate experiences to ladies.

He was meant to talk about roses and ponies. He should be romancing her, since this was the first time they were supposed to be meeting after a long separation. Instead, he was scaring her with visions of mummies.

"You were in Egypt?" Catherine, on the other hand, sounded enchanted.

"Yes, a few years back. It was an exhilarating experience. A man I travelled with was bitten by an asp. He died."

While Catherine gasped, Emma walked away. She had never realised her cousin had such a bloodthirsty soul.

Chapter 14

"My dear child, you should not be wasting your time with me when your betrothed is in the same room. Why don't you sit with him?" the Duchess admonished.

"You are hardly old, aunty, and I believe you are prettier than all the ladies present here. As for the Earl, I . . . " Emma paused, unable to come up with an excuse. She had taken a seat next to the Duchess hoping to avoid that very question.

The Duchess patted her hand sympathetically. "I think time apart from your betrothed has made things awkward between you. One forms an intimacy through letters, and when you meet the person in the flesh, you don't know how to behave. Give it time, and things will get back to normal before you know it."

Emma was grateful for the excuse and heartily agreed with her aunt's reading of the situation.

Dinner was announced, and they all trooped into the dining room to find the Duke already present at the head of the table.

While the first course of cold soup and duck salad was being served, the Duke engaged Lord Raikes in conversation.

It seemed to be going well until Catherine interrupted him, "You have had him to yourself long enough, father." She tilted her head in Lord Raikes direction, "Now, My Lord, I have a question for you that no one seems to be asking. How is it that you have black hair when we all know the Earl is, in fact, blonde?"

The entire table froze, cocking their ears to hear the reply.

Instead of looking uncomfortable, Lord Raikes leaned back and smiled ruefully, "Alas, that is an embarrassing story, and I was hoping to avoid telling it. But I see it is necessary to do so now."

Emma sat up straighter. So the Earl had not forgotten, and they had concocted a story. If it were embarrassing, then it would be more believable."

Lord Raikes continued, "I was staying with an aunt of mine who happens to have seven children. My nephew, who is eight, spent the entire week following me around. I confess to being absent minded at times, and he found me in a distracted mood one day. A particular business matter was bothering me, and it was hard to think with so many children running in and out of the house. So forgive me for what I did next."

Here he paused to take a sip of wine and then continued, "He asked me how he could take revenge on his tutor, who, he assured me, was an absolute tyrant. I had, during my own childhood days, taken a passionate interest in chemistry. I gave him a formula for hair dye which I had used on my own governess, who had long red curly locks. She had been extremely proud of it. The dye is easy to make and the materials are readily available amongst household supplies. Now, you can guess what happened next. My dear clever nephew decided to dye my hair while I slept, to ascertain that it actually worked. You see, the lad could not imagine that an adult would give him such a beautiful bit of mischief. My aunt threw me out, and I do not blame her."

"It suits you. Why, I cannot imagine you with anything but black hair," Prudence remarked.

"It will stay dark for only three more weeks. It will eventually fade away. It is not permanent," he smiled back.

Emma sighed in relief, while Catherine looked disappointed.

"I am sorry," Catherine whispered to Emma while the Duke once again engaged Lord Raikes in conversation.

"For what, Cat?"

"Emmy, I was an absolute beast to your fiancé. I was angry with the way he treated me on his arrival. He is very arrogant just like you said, and he rubs me the wrong way . . . but I truly should have made more of an effort to like him."

"He takes some getting used to," she replied, secretly wondering how she would deal with him herself. That man had barely spoken two words to her all evening, and people were bound to notice soon. His arrogance made Richard look angelic in comparison.

They were to dance that evening, and for that purpose, they retired to the music room after dinner.

Catherine sat playing the piano and the Duchess hinted to Lord

Raikes that he should open the dance with Emma. It was a broad enough hint for him to comprehend its meaning.

Accordingly, Emma found herself dancing and finally alone with him.

"You need to be careful, My Lord. Everyone has noticed that you have barely spoken to me since your arrival. Please remember, I am your fiancée."

Lord Raikes replied apologetically, "Richard has put me in such a difficult situation. I do not deal well with strangers. Forgive me for not paying you enough attention. I will remedy it immediately."

"You are forgiven, My Lord. Now, is there anything I need to know? How did the meeting with the Duke go? Did he suspect anything?"

"No, I think it is too early to tell if the Duke suspects. He did not interrogate me as I have only arrived today. He will no doubt ask me some questions in the morning. He has requested my presence in his study."

"I see, and have you met Richard?"

"I did. I stopped at the village first, and he briefed me. He wants us to take a walk in the morning after breakfast. That will have to wait now, as I have to meet the Duke. In the afternoon, we can go for a stroll, and if your chaperone will be kind enough to leave us alone, we can try and meet Richard."

"Oh, I will ask Catherine to engage Lady Babbage. Escaping her will not be a problem."

"Catherine seems to dislike me."

"You mistook her for a maid, My Lord. No wonder she is offended."

"Oh, no, not again! I truly think only maids should be allowed to wear grey. How is a man to tell the difference between a lady and a maid if they both wear the same colour?"

"She wore a dove grey silk dress, and even if she wore a sack, it would be hard to confuse her with a maid. Her face is aristocratic and her hands soft as butter."

"Yes, I can't imagine how I made such a gaffe. She is beautiful. Is she engaged?"

Emma wanted to laugh. Here was another complication they did not need.

"She is unclaimed, My Lord. Though, please remember, you are not. You are supposed to be engaged to me."

"I am hardly likely to forget," he replied, staring at the corner where Catherine sat playing the Piano. After a few moments of silence, he sighed and said, "She plays well."

Emma sighed as well and allowed herself to be led in the direction of the pianoforte.

He danced with all the ladies present, and knowing how uncomfortable he was, she was pleased that he had managed to charm all members of her sex present. The fact that he was extremely handsome made things somewhat easier for him. He barely spoke a word, yet the women made up for it. He was considered a good listener, and what woman does not love a listening man.

In contrast, his dance with Catherine was conducted in silence. They could not hold a conversation without arguing, so they both thought it prudent to keep their mouth shut in each other's company.

❖ ❖ ❖

"Are you sure you want to marry him?"

"Cat, we have been over this for two hours. Yes, I want to marry the Earl . . . now can I have my breakfast?"

"But he is so different from what you said. He dislikes company, I could see it in his face the entire night. He is polite, but his conversations seem stiff and forced."

"You have just met him. I am sorry he mistook you for a maid, but he is a very nice man. Give him time, he will grow on you. You cannot judge a man after one meal."

"I don't know why I am reacting so strongly. This is not like me. I always give people the benefit of the doubt. But my gut tells me something is not right. Why, his behaviour towards you was almost cold."

"He was embarrassed. He wanted to spend time with me alone, but it was difficult with so many present eyeing our every move. We both felt unnatural, and I am sure things will be better today."

"I suppose you are right," said Catherine doubtfully.

"We are to take a walk in the afternoon. Will you join us?" Emma asked.

"Yes, and keep the chaperone away," she added slyly.

"Thank you. Now, I am going to eat, and I don't want to hear another word from you until I am done."

Catherine left her cousin to her breakfast and went to the library.

It was a large room filled with books and the smell of leather and tobacco.

It reminded her of her father and how as a child she used to sit and listen to him read in his deep baritone voice. It comforted her, and she still missed those winter days by the fireside. Now she found the same solace in books, and her love for the room grew as the years sped by.

She walked towards the shelf searching its titles, when a cough alerted her to another presence.

Lord Raikes' head peered at her from the side of a cherry coloured high backed chair. The sun streamed in through the window striking the back of his head making his hair gleam like shards of black ice. A dark shadow had appeared on his jawline making him look far handsomer than he had on his arrival.

She greeted him, her lips pinched and her eyes wary.

Instead of replying he walked up to her and took her hand, "I am deeply sorry if I offended you in any way, Lady Arden."

Flustered, she stared into his dark blue eyes. She had not expected him to approach so boldly.

"Forgive me, My Lord, I behaved badly as well last night. My pride was hurt, and I lashed out at you."

He smiled; his eyes crinkled in amusement as he answered, "Shall we part as friends and forget the entire episode?"

"Yes, that would please me, My Lord."

He briefly pressed her hand before continuing, "I often find comfort in libraries. They all hold the scent of books and leather, and apart from the differences in furnishing they remain the cosiest of rooms in any household."

"I agree," she replied, trying to pull her hand free. He refused to relinquish his firm hold.

"You came in search of a book," he continued, as if unaware of the gentle tugging. "Allow me to direct you towards some titles suited for a lady's perusal. You can discuss my choice in the afternoon when we take our walk."

She snatched her hand back, her earlier softening mood rapidly turning to furious anger. His tone was so authoritative that it irked her.

"I can choose my own books, thank you. I do not need advice, and I am allowed to read what I please. My father has never resorted to dictate my tastes or steer me towards literature that is considered suitable for ladies. He believes in broadening my education and allowing me to judge what is appropriate for me. As for discussing anything in the afternoon, I am afraid you forget that you will be occupied with Emma, who is your fiancée and whom you have not seen for several weeks. You would hardly want to waste your time discoursing with me."

His dark hooded eyes searched her face, his expression speculative. He didn't seem offended by her sudden outburst . . . but looks could be deceptive.

She dropped her lashes, unable to hold his gaze for long.

With half a smile, he turned away to glance at the books lining the shelves. His eyebrow rose when he spotted a partially concealed copy of a book a heartbeat away from where Catherine stood.

He frowned, "Do you mean to tell me that your father allows you to take any book from this library. Are none of the titles forbidden to you?"

"Yes, he has never sought to dictate my reading habits," she lied boldly. She was not allowed to venture into certain sections of the library, but she was loath to admit it to the blasted, arrogant man.

He strode over to the shelf and pulled out the title he had been eyeing. He turned the book towards her and softly asked, "And what, pray, is your opinion on this particular piece of poetry?"

Catherine stared in mortification at a partially nude woman gracing the covers of 'Ovid'. Her cheeks reddened, and she dared not lift her eyes up to the laughing man in front of her.

She could neither deny nor brazenly agree that she had read it. Instead, she took the coward's way out and fled.

His laughter followed her as she raced out of the room.

Chapter 15

It took all Catherine's nerve to appear before the party that afternoon. She had to splash her face with cold water multiple times to cool her heated cheeks. Unlike her cousin, she had always been demure and shy. Her strange behaviour and outspokenness with the Earl alarmed her.

While Emma would have laughed off the incident, she wanted to crawl into bed and hide. It was her pride that forced her to face the man. She was the Duke's daughter, after all, and no mocking smile would have her feigning illness over such a trifling incident.

Accordingly, she found herself walking towards the garden in her pale blue walking dress. A cream wrap around her shoulders reminded her that summer was truly over.

Lord Raikes glanced at the fetching vision Catherine made. Emma held on to his arm as they strolled, but his eyes kept returning to her cousin.

Catherine resolutely kept her eyes downcast and had not even looked at him once.

Her soft replies to his greeting irritated him. He wanted to take hold of her chin and force her to meet his eyes.

"Look, the leaves are turning gold, My Lord," Prudence said, breaking his train of thought.

Prudence was another reason why he was annoyed. She had blatantly thrown herself at him, rudely ignoring the other girls. She clung to his other arm while he tried hard to forget she was there.

"Yes, they are turning gold, but that is to be expected, for autumn is setting in," he replied blandly.

"Would you like to go for a ride, My Lord? The stable is well provided with some excellent mounts to choose from. We should take advantage of the last few days of warmth," Prudence asked.

"I doubt Lady Babbage would want to sit upon a horse in this lifetime," said Emma, glancing back at the older woman strolling behind them with Catherine. "Besides, the day is not warm. The rain last night seems to have washed away all traces of summer."

"Why can't we go on our own? The Duke needs to venture out to London and realise the changes that have occurred in society. Why we need to be watched so strictly is beyond me. I, for one, am willing to take the chance and face the Duke's wrath, if you are," Prudence replied, fluttering her lashes up at him.

"I am afraid I will have to decline your tempting offer, as I would like to spend some time with my fiancé. I have not seen her for almost a fortnight," he said politely.

The broad hint to leave them alone was not lost on Prudence, and she shot a scathing look in Emma's direction. But even she could think of no good reason to hang on to his arm any longer, so she dropped her hand and turned to engage Catherine in conversation.

"How are we to escape them? Catherine can handle Lady Babbage, but Prudence has her eyes set on you. She will not let us disappear so easily." Emma whispered.

"I think we may not be able to meet Richard . . . Wait . . . isn't that him mucking about in that flower bed? Good Lord, I had never imagined I would ever see him tending so lovingly to daisies," he replied laughing.

She scowled in response and strode towards the Earl, pulling Lord Raikes along.

"Good evening, miss. Nice day," the Earl said, setting aside his spade.

"We cannot get rid of them," Emma hurriedly spoke. "Can you see me tonight in my room?"

At Lord Raikes' horrified gasp, the Earl grinned. "Not what you imagine, William. I have been perfectly honourable, contrary to my nature. Close your mouth man, and stop behaving like an outraged virgin."

Prudence's high pitched voice interrupted their hushed conversation,

"You have found your gardener. I must tell you, My Lord, Emma has developed a grand passion for gardening. Why, she is never far from the head gardener at any time."

"I am happy to find my fiancée taking an interest in plants. I am partial to them myself. If it were not for herbs, I would not be alive today. Why, when I was in India I came down with yellow fever and — " began Lord Raikes

"I am a little cold, My Lord," Emma cut in. She was pleased that Lord Raikes had tried to defend her interest, but her mood had rapidly plunged once she realised that meeting Richard would be even more difficult now with the presence of Lord Raikes.

Prudence would not allow them breathing room in the coming days. She also had no interest in hearing him talk of pestilence, diseases, or exotic animals.

Lord Raikes immediately took her meaning and seeing the look of frustration on her face, he gently steered her towards the house.

He said, "I think it will be easier for our gardener to meet you at night, for if he is found strolling the hallways, he can always say I requested his presence. I can invent a terrible fever that I caught in some exotic country and only a certain type of herb can relieve the symptoms. Since he is the head gardener, who better to call upon for assistance? I can even make the ailment embarrassing, so no one dares to question too closely."

Emma smiled at him in genuine delight for the first time. He was worthy of being a friend to Richard. Why, Lord William Raikes had the potential to be as evil as the Earl himself.

Emma could finally see herself liking the man.

❖ ❖ ❖

The real Earl watched Emma's face light up at something his friend had whispered into her ear. Watching her laughing, he wondered uneasily if he had made a mistake by bringing his handsome friend into the equation. William was not only rich, but he was also famous.

Irritably, he yanked a perfect daisy from its roots and flung it away. He would have to warn the man to keep his hands off her and to stop making her laugh or to whisper anything in her ear . . . Why, he would tell him not to speak a word to Emma ever again.

He stood up, and disregarding his character as an old man, briskly walked towards a pond he knew off. It was hidden from the view of the main house and edged with weeping willows. The whole effect was sad yet beautiful.

He chose a particularly morose looking tree, whose branches almost touched the water shimmering below. He climbed high enough so he wouldn't be spotted and pulled out his tobacco.

He wanted to sit in peace and not be discovered while he chose the best and most horrendous words to describe his best friend.

His creative mental process was disrupted when the sound of voices floated up towards him. He quickly moved his position to further conceal himself from prying eyes.

"I need more time," someone whined.

"I have given you almost a year. If you think you can attract the Earl with your pathetic attempts, then you are mistaken. You are already wearing gowns one year out of date. Don't think I do not know that half your clothes are altered to mimic the latest styles. I could never forget that hideous orange colour, no matter what you fashion it into."

"That is not true! I have plenty of new clothes. I went to Paris and had an entire wardrobe made."

"My dear child, you went to Paris a year and a half ago. Some relative took pity on you and provided you with a few measly dresses. Since England is so behind the times, naturally those dresses seem the height of fashion right now. But what will you do next year? You have been out for a while now, and not even in Paris could you catch a man. You are getting desperate, and we both know why."

"I am sure papa can provide me with another season, and when I do marry, I promise to pay you handsomely."

"Your father has no more money. He is swimming in debt, and you know it. He will not be able to provide for another season. I doubt you will ever marry well, but for the moment your secret is safe."

"Thank you . . ."

The voice cut in harshly, "Don't thank me until you hear me out. I saw a pretty brooch that you wore last night. It took my fancy. Rubies, if I am not mistaken. Bring it to me, and you may have another month."

"But that is not mine! My grandmother let me borrow it. I am to return it to her. I cannot give that to you."

"Well, then we have nothing more to say to each other."

"No wait, I have pearls . . ."

"I *want* the brooch."

"Fine, I . . . I will bring it to you tonight."

"Thank you, and next time I will not meet you like this. I prefer to keep my transactions discreet. Leave a note in my work basket when you have anything of value to give me, else do not bother seeking me out."

The Earl sat puffing his pipe as he went over the conversation. The voice had been unmistakable. It had been Prudence begging for more time from Lady Babbage. He had been right. That old woman was up to something.

It was clear that she had some damning evidence against the girl. He was surprised to learn that the Barkers were in financial difficulty. They seemed well dressed, though Emma had mentioned Mrs Barker behaving just as desperate as her daughter.

Was Lady Babbage blackmailing the mother and daughter, or was Mrs Barker simply willing to be the Duke's mistress to restore their financial situation?

The entire incident left a bad taste in his mouth. How could that woman be so heartless and demand payment from someone so young? He had never liked Prudence, from what little he had seen or heard of her, but all he felt at the moment was pity for the girl and disgust at Lady Babbage's behaviour. He debated telling Emma.

Emma would be just as disgusted, but would she be able to hide her feelings from the vicious woman? It would be harder for her to pretend. Blackmailing a gardener for some odd job was different from demanding payment from a helpless young girl.

Whatever indiscretion Prudence had committed, it did not seem fair that Lady Babbage held it over her head like a sword.

He extinguished his pipe in distaste. He could not tell Emma, at least not yet. She would never be able to treat the Lady courteously, or keep up the pretence of being unaware of what was going on in the house.

He would have to alert William and ask him to keep an eye on things.

❖ ❖ ❖

"Do I need to beg your forgiveness once again, Lady Arden?"
Catherine missed her lips and instead wetted her chin with the tea.
"Here," Lord Raikes said, producing a snow-white handkerchief.
She glanced at him questioningly.
"The tea may dribble down onto your dress. I am partial to that colour on your skin and would not like the cloth stained," he replied.
Mortified, she grabbed the handkerchief and quickly wiped away

the liquid.

"You did not answer my first question. Do I need to apologise? I had not meant to tease you this morning. No, don't try and convince me that it was nothing . . . you have not looked at me once since the incident, not during our stroll, or through the entire dinner."

Catherine glanced around looking for an escape.

"Do I frighten you?"

"No!" she snapped, her eyes flashing angrily as she finally met his gaze.

"That's better. I will try and never tease you again."

She nodded distractedly, trying to inch away from him.

He had sat next to her as soon as Lady Babbage had retired for bed. No one else seemed inclined to end the night early, and she had been enjoying the festive feel the newcomer had brought with him.

Everyone wanted to talk and to flirt. Somehow, with the sun setting, people felt the thrill of risk, and prolonging the bedtime added to the adventure. They changed and grew bolder as the hours sped by. The politeness that had dictated the conversations all day seemed to slowly ebb and skate the bounds of propriety.

It was the wine, she concluded, that loosened tongues and put odd thoughts in one's head.

"I never realised how well green compliments blue. I confess, I have never noticed how beautiful this material is, it skims the body taunting one's imagination," he said, touching the edge of her moss silk skirt.

She leapt up, her own light blue eyes glaring into darker ones.

"I think I would like more tea, My Lord." She turned away, only to whirl back around and say, "I cannot sit here and listen to you speak so. How can you? When you know you are to marry my cousin. I implore you to keep your smooth tongue to yourself. I have not been in London or out in society; hence, do not know how to play games of this sort. Think of me as a country bumpkin rather than a sophisticated Londoner, please, and choose your words carefully."

He rose to his feet, and a brief flash of pain crossed his face.

"I think you are a beautiful bluestocking, and I wish circumstances had been different. Please trust me, and not think of me so harshly. I know everything against me seems black right now, but do not hate me just yet. I implore you to give me time to explain."

"Even if you were not betrothed to my cousin, I would still find it hard to ignore your arrogance. In every tone and every word you speak, there is a command. I am afraid hate is too harsh a word to use. Indifference is what I truly feel for you and concern for Emma. That girl has lost her head over a handsome face," she said, walking away.

❖ ❖ ❖

Catherine stared at the snowy white handkerchief in her hand. She had forgotten to return it in her agitation to get away. Now she would have to go back and face him again.

She glanced at the fire burning in the grate and contemplated throwing it in. It would be childish, she finally conceded.

That man was a rogue. He dared to flirt openly with her and say things no gentleman would utter. Her cheeks burned, and furious tears threatened to spill from her eyes. She hated the man and wondered how long she would have to suffer his odious presence. She seemed to embarrass herself every time she met him.

A dark patch at the edge of the handkerchief captured her attention for a moment. She squinted at the embroidery at the corner of the cloth and blinked away the tears to see more clearly.

She frowned. The initials were W.S.R; why did the Earl have W.S.R sewn into his handkerchief. Should it not be R.A.H? Her initial suspicion returned.

Was that man truly Richard Hamilton or someone else? He did not match the description Emma had given her. He behaved like an Earl and had the lordly habits down pat, yet her uneasiness did not go away.

From the very beginning, something had not seemed right. She wondered if Emma had a lover, and this was her way of introducing him to the Duke. She could have intercepted the letter and begged this man to pretend to be the Earl. Maybe her aim was to show how much better than the Earl this man truly was.

She grimaced in annoyance. Her imagination was taking flight; as if Emma would practice such a deceit. If anything, it would anger the Duke if the truth came out, and he would forbid her cousin to have anything to do with the man.

Why, she ruthlessly asked herself, was she trying to convince herself that the Earl was an imposter?

She had imagined the Earl as a male version of her cousin; fun loving, bold and charming, with no interest in anything but the outdoors.

She had expected a boy. Instead, she was faced with an intelligent man who was well-read, interesting, deep and an introvert. No wonder she was confused. He was nothing like what her cousin had portrayed him to be. She had not been prepared, and that was it. That was the only reason for her antagonism. Their meeting had started off on a wrong footing, and what with one thing and another, the situation had become worse.

She did not think she could be friends with him any longer, though, for Emma's sake, she would be polite and keep her distance.

His flirting must have charmed more sophisticated women, while she had only been subjected to a few immature efforts from the village lads. He had taken her by surprise, his words shocking her.

With growing mortification, she realised she looked like an even bigger fool now than she had with tea dribbling down her chin.

Maybe flirting so boldly was all the rage in London. She had been living in a secluded village and been unaware of how society had progressed. He must have simply been saying things that were expected of him, and she had overreacted, taking his meaning to be more than he had intended. Perhaps he had no interest in her, and her outburst would have only highlighted her misplaced pride.

The stupid handkerchief could have had his great aunt's name embroidered for all she knew. Angrily, she turned and left for bed without wishing anyone present goodnight.

Chapter 16

"I want you to stay away from William."

Emma stepped out of the Earl's arm in surprise. He had met her in her room again, and she had leaped into his arms happily. Now she searched his face and noticed the tight lines around his mouth.

"Why?"

"Because he is a rake and a blackguard, and you are not safe with him! You do not know the things he has done. He is ten times worse than me. He has no honest bone in his body, and he will compromise you before you can . . , why are you laughing?"

"He is your best friend, and as for him compromising me, he barely speaks to me. He is obsessed with my cousin. I have to continuously remind him that I am his fiancée."

"*Pretend* fiancée."

"Yes, alright, *pretend* fiancée, and I think we should be worried about him compromising Catherine under the Duke's very own roof. I have never seen my poor cousin blush so much as she does in his company. I thought he was a boring old professor, but he must be saying some truly outrageous things to her to have her so flustered."

"Oh, dear."

"Richard," she said giggling, "you sound like my mamma. You had the disapproving tone down perfectly."

"Well, since I will be related to her soon enough, I feel obligated to protect Catherine from that scoundrel."

"What brought about this sudden change? I thought you were best friends, and according to you, he is absolutely wonderful. If you did not want me to interact with him, then why in the world did you choose him for this charade? I cannot act my role if I am not allowed to even speak to him. The Duke, for one, will find it decidedly odd."

"That was before . . . "

"Before what?"

"Never mind. Just hear me out. You must chaperone your cousin, and ignore my rant of staying away from him. He is a wily fox, and we need to keep Catherine's virtue safe. Otherwise, we will have more to worry about than the Duke discovering my identity. I am not so sure I would win in a duel against him. He practices every morning, did you know? I watched him, and his aim is dead on at fifty paces."

"I think William is a gentleman, and you had a decidedly better opinion of him a few days ago. I am truly interested to know what changed your mind."

The Earl stooped to kiss her to silence her questions. He did not want to admit his jealousy.

She laughingly tried to fend him off to continue her line of thought, but he held her hands in an iron grip allowing no room for escape. She finally gave in, and her laughter faded as desire mounted.

A knock at the door had them both leap apart in shock.

"Who is it?" Emma called.

"Raikes"

"That good for nothing . . . " the Earl's tirade was halted by Emma who quickly opened the door.

"I called him", she replied apologetically, "I thought we could discuss things more easily here."

"You, my dear, will never entertain any man other than me in your bedroom. Is that clear?" the Earl growled angrily.

Seeing the furious look on his face she nodded meekly.

He turned to face Lord Raikes,

"You, get out and stay out. I will meet you in your room. We can talk there, and you can update Emma tomorrow during daylight, with at least three chaperones present. Is that clear?"

"Yes, Richard," he said in a brilliant imitation of a meek young lady. He threw in a curtsey at the end.

Emma dissolved into giggles, and the Earl slammed the door shut on his friend.

❖ ❖ ❖

"At least you will have a glass of decent malt for me every night. I have never appreciated such small luxuries before," the Earl muttered.

"You can sleep on the couch," Lord Raikes offered.

"That Pickering would notice. I think the Duke has asked him to keep an eye on me, and he does a good imitation of a faithful hound. I have half a mind to lure him away with double the pay."

"Just so you can order him around as he has been ordering you about the past few days?"

"Exactly," the Earl replied, taking a swig from the glass.

"You do know I would never dare think of Emma in any other way than your bride . . . don't you?" he asked seriously.

"I know, I am sorry I reacted so strongly earlier. It is just that once you find someone you . . . you care about, jealousy is not far behind. I want to possess her, and I know how barbarian that sounds, believe me," the Earl said ruefully. "But one day you will understand. It is part of the reason for the charade. I want to marry her and do the honourable thing. Not just because I desire her physically but because I want to have her by my side, sharing my life, my home and my family. I want the people I value in my life to know her and love her as she deserves."

"I never thought I would see the day when my friend would admit to being in love."

"I never said I loved her!"

"You did not have to," Lord Raikes replied smiling.

"Enough about me, tell me how do you find being in love?"

"In love! You must be joking, I just met her."

"Yes, Prudence is a lovely girl, you can't do better than her."

"Pru . . . " he spluttered, then seeing the Earl laughing, scowled, "I would not touch her with a barge pole."

The Earl sobered, feeling sorry for the unfortunate girl once more. He related the events of the afternoon and told him of Lady Babbage's attempts to blackmail.

Lord Raikes frowned and said, "Lady Babbage seems to be genuinely fond of Catherine, yet I am not surprised to hear of her unpleasant activities. She reminds me of an aunt I had. A woman who appeared wonderfully calm and yet underneath the surface she was so steeped in bitterness and anger that she ended up killing her own child and hanging in the gallows for it."

"William, Lady Babbage, frightens me, and I do not mind admitting it. I chanced a glimpse of Prudence's face as she watched Lady Babbage leave, and the hatred I saw was disturbing. She has pushed the girl to the edge, and I don't know how many others. I have a suspicion she may be trying her tricks with the Duke as well. This whole house seems to be a disaster waiting to happen. Things may get ugly, and I trust you to keep Em safe."

"I am honoured, and I will do my best, Richard. Though, I do hope you are wrong about things getting worse."

"I don't think I am wrong. My next step is to throw myself in Lady Babbage's path and see what she wants from an old gardener. I wonder what job she has for me. It cannot be straightforward, and her demands may throw more clues our way."

Lord Raikes smiled. His friend looked more delighted with a chance to solve a mystery than worried about any impending danger. Gardening was an excellent occupation for the Earl, no matter his complaints.

❖ ❖ ❖

The day dawned grey, wet, and thundery. The storm had the entire household imprisoned inside.

Emma was miserable since she would miss her daily stroll.

The women along with Mr Barker sat in the breakfast room, reluctant to leave its warmth.

"I am sure my nose will turn blue if I step out of this room. The hallways are so drafty, and with the slightest dip in temperature the walls turn to ice," the Duchess commented.

"I prefer my own modest home. These great mansions are splendid to look at but impractical to live in. You should acquire a smaller place. I am sure the Duke will be pleased with doing away with the expense of keeping this grand home in order," Mrs Barker replied.

"I, for one, love this house, with all its shivers and whistles. The Duke needs to maintain this grandness, as you call it, because his status requires him to do so. He has responsibilities to his tenants, and he cannot abandon hundreds of people that depend on him for their livelihood. Pass me the teapot, Cat," Emma said irritably.

"Here you go. Does anyone know where the Earl and father are? I have not seen them all morning," Catherine asked.

"They had decided to go fishing today, but I am sure this horrible rain has them ensconced in the study. Personally, I find fishing a dreadful bore. You wake up at dawn and trudge your way up to a pond or lake and sit in utter silence waiting for a catch. The entire process leaves you cold, sleepy, and depressed. Now, hunting is more exciting," Mr Barker replied.

"Ah, some fresh, hot coffee," the Duchess interrupted, eyeing a maid entering the room with a cleverly balanced tray of coffee, tea, and lemon cake.

"I don't think I want to move. I have eaten so much, yet another cup sounds heavenly. This room is rather warm, but I think it is the knowledge of the torrent outside that makes us feel as if we should curl up with a posset in the corner," Emma said gloomily.

They sat in silence, having nothing more to offer.

Catherine wondered how she could enliven everyone's mood. She stared around the room, racking her brains for some interesting game they could play without anyone having to move an inch.

"Eek!" Prudence shrieked into the calm. Her face had turned deathly white, and she slowly lifted her finger and pointed to a spot near the door.

"Eek!" Mr Barker and Catherine echoed, spotting the source of Prudence's screech.

"Good lord, it's . . . it's a mouse," the Duchess whispered in horror.

Slowly and carefully, so as not to startle the creature, everyone climbed onto their respective chairs.

Mr Barker went a step further by launching himself onto the table. They stood watching the animal, not daring to breathe.

"It hasn't moved. It is just sitting there," Emma whispered, after a few minutes.

"I cannot see," Mrs Barker complained, "what is it like?"

"Brown and small and . . . twitchy," Emma replied.

"I think he is moving," Catherine, who was closest to the creature, muttered. "Yes, he is . . . see, he is turning around, and now — " She froze.

" . . . It is facing us," finished Emma.

Everyone paused, eyes riveted towards the mouse, waiting for it to make its next move.

After another minute of stillness on both sides, Emma finally said, "How do you know it is a he?"

"It looks like a he," Catherine replied.

"He is sort of cute," Prudence said apologetically, "Look at his wee face, with his little quivering whiskers, staring up at us with those tiny paws outstretched."

"Now I am sure it is a 'he', since we have Prudence already in love with the thing," Emma breathed into her cousin's ear.

"I don't know, he is sort of adorable," Catherine replied and then added loudly, "he looks hungry."

"He does, the poor thing. The cold outside must have forced him to join us. Do you think we should feed him?" the Duchess asked. No one moved from their position.

Finally, Mrs Barker, tired of not being able to see the thing for herself, decided to climb onto the breakfast table and have a closer look. She carefully placed her knees on the edge of the table. She heaved herself on top and straightened unsteadily. She wobbled her way down the table, avoiding the various dishes and cups.

She had gone a few paces when she misjudged the fourth step. Her foot landed in the dish of butter, and she went down with a crash. Her skirts flew up, and her arms flapped in the air.

Concerned and horrified faces were momentarily diverted from the mouse.

Mrs Barker's voice came from within her voluminous skirts flung over her head, "I have an idea, why don't we throw a bit of cheese to it?"

Relieved giggles erupted around the table. They turned back to look towards the door.

The mouse had frozen in fright from the noise of the crash. Not a whisker trembled as it sat exactly where he had sat for the last ten minutes.

Prudence, being closest to the cheese, broke off a piece and handed it to Catherine, who was in the best position to feed the mouse.

"What should I do?" she asked nervously.

"Just throw it in the general direction. Not too close to it, mind you, or you will frighten it away from the food. See that spot near the side table? Now, aim it there, and hopefully the poor starved thing will smell it," Mr Barker ordered, from his safe position on top of the table.

He was the only man about, and he considered it his duty to lead the proceedings in the correct manner.

Catherine bit her lip and flung the cheese towards the intended spot. Everyone watched the cheese as it soared high up towards the ceiling and then fell. It fell not at its intended spot but a few paces away from where Catherine stood.

A collective sigh echoed in the room. A sigh full of many meanings, a sigh that spoke of their relief that the cheese didn't smack the mouse on its head, a sigh that was sorrowful of the fact that the cheese was nowhere close to the mouse. A sigh that soon turned into nervous grunts and squeals as the mouse leaped in fright at this new form of attack.

The mouse paused mid-flight, its nose twitching and its eyes questioning. It gathered its courage and moved towards the cheese, taking cautious steps.

The Duchess smiled in delight and then frowned; the mouse had reached the cheese, but that meant it was now closer to their table.

They watched, stomachs churning in anticipation as it sniffed the morsel and . . . then the door banged open.

"Did it get the cheese?"

The Duke walked in to catch this last query, with the Earl following him in. He stared at all the ladies standing on top of the chairs, and his right eye twitched at the sight of Mrs Barker sitting amid the breakfast food with her skirts ballooning out awkwardly. Mr Barker was hurriedly assisting his wife.

The Duke finally spoke,

"Is this a new fashion in London of eating breakfast? One must no longer sit on chairs but stand on them? And what in the world is Mrs Barker doing . . . I am a little afraid to ask."

"A mouse, father," Catherine replied meekly.

"A *mouse*?" he asked, staring at Mr Barker.

Mr Barker turned bright red.

"And who was asking for cheese?"

"The mouse," Emma spoke, embarrassed.

"I see, the mouse was asking for cheese."

"No, oh! You have it all mixed up. It was like this. We saw a mouse and were frightened, but then we all felt sorry for the creature. He was a fetching thing, so we were just attempting to feed him a bit of cheese when you walked in." Prudence explained.

"I see and did you name him as well?" he asked in amusement, and at the abashed shakes of heads, he added, "I will ask Pickering to come and take care of our uninvited guest . . . who seems to have disappeared at the moment. And no, I do not want to know how Mrs Barker came to be a part of the meal. Hamilton, join me in the library for a cup of coffee."

Pickering arrived shortly after the departure of the Duke and Lord Raikes. He was told not to kill the mouse but put it away in a safe place.

"We are all very attached to the dear creature. Leave some water and food by its side," the Duchess directed.

Pickering stared at the various lords and ladies standing on top of tables and chairs, presumably because of that very dear creature.

For the first and last time since joining the Duke's household an expression crossed his face. Unfortunately, no one present could decipher what that emotion was. It was a rare opportunity often lamented upon being lost.

Chapter 17

"What happened to it?" Lord Raikes asked Catherine.

He had searched the entire house and found her alone in the music room. He entered uninvited.

"The '*it*' is a 'he'. Pickering came armed with a broom, a paper bag, and a stable hand. They spent some time chasing it around the room, and finally he was cornered near the chimney. We have been assured he is safe," she replied primly, moving to shut the piano.

"Stay, I would like to hear you play," he said, catching her hand.

"Emma is in the morning room," she replied instead, pulling her hand back.

"But I would like to know her cousin better."

"You may, once you are married. I will spend considerable time at your home after the occasion, so you can further our acquaintance then."

"I would like us to be friends now, for Emma's sake. She would want the two people closest to her to at least like each other," he said shrewdly.

She hesitated briefly and then sat back down on the piano seat.

"What would you like to speak of?" she finally asked.

"We have something in common . . . books. We both enjoy reading. Surely we can find a common author that we like?"

"I doubt my reading list would suit your refined taste. According to you we women should only read what is deemed appropriate for us. I do not think you would like such authors."

"Name an author you like, and I will tell you what I think of him."

"I prefer to talk of subjects rather than authors. Travel accounts are far more instructive and colourful than the dry pages of other texts. I envy you. You, being a man, can travel where you please, while I have to find my adventure in the pages of books."

He looked at her wistful face and suddenly felt the urge to pack his bags and take her along with him to some exotic land. He cleared his throat as he answered,

"Have you heard of an author," he paused and then continued "W.S. Raikes?"

"I have read one account of his trip to India. Father keeps some of his books in the library."

"What do you think of his works?" he asked nervously.

"I think he must be an arrogant, selfish, and an extremely annoying man. I imagine he is a hundred years old with a bald head and crooked teeth. On his travels, he must carry a spy glass and peer at everything and anything that comes across his way, always remaining the distant observer."

"You got all that from his writing?" he asked angrily, and then seeing the startled look on her face softened his tone and said, "Why would you draw such harsh conclusions?"

"He writes well, when I can understand it. In every sentence, I feel he is trying to show how much better he is than the rest of us. He uses obscure words that I can never find in dictionaries. He fails to realise that not all of us have travelled to so many countries, and hence our vocabulary is limited. I understand French and Latin, but how an English reader is meant to understand Spanish, Italian, Greek, and goodness knows what else, is beyond me. He writes for old, stodgy professors or his fellow travellers. The rest of us mortals are left feeling foolish."

"Perhaps he writes for himself?"

"Then why get it published? The whole point of a book is to entertain or instruct. He does neither, for I cannot decipher half of it."

"Surely his accounts, if not entertaining, are at least instructive? Sometimes it is inevitable that one uses words from certain languages, since our own limited language cannot describe the intent clearly. A whole plethora of emotions cannot be put down on paper if one is limited to one script. Besides, I am sure the act of looking up the obscure words he mentions taught you something."

"I forgot the words as soon as I looked them up. It would annoy people if I started speaking like an old university professor. As for instruction, he does not in all his travel accounts mention anything about women. He completely ignores their existence. How is that possible? He cannot be that blind, and they form the other and very crucial half of society."

"Perhaps he does so to protect the modesty of the English mind. Cultures differ and if not understood properly can become a source of misplaced humour. He keeps the women out of his works to protect the women of all cultures and to maintain a level of respect that comes with the unknown."

"You are making no sense. The author needs to respect his readers as well, to allow them the sensitivity to judge for themselves. An educated man or woman would not deride other cultures simply because they are different. I think this W. S. Raikes does not like women and does not consider them important. He must have been jilted sometime in his life, and I applaud the woman for her good sense. I also think that he is your bosom friend, since you seem to be getting angry on his behalf."

He stared at her in shock and anger. She had touched a nerve when she mentioned the author being jilted.

He had at eighteen been in love with a woman who had spurned him for an older, more successful man. He would have come into his title too late for it to suit her. It was that very reason which had prompted him to escape England and travel.

He had not realised his old hurt still affected his writing. He had wanted to hear words of praise, since he was lauded by his peers for his works. No one had criticized him so bitterly, and the underlying truth hurt him.

"Just because you are not intelligent enough to understand his works, which are well received by the general, educated public, you stoop to malign his character. I had asked you about his works, not an analysis of the man's personality. You have never met him, you know nothing of him, and yet you judge him. You have never ventured out of this tiny village, and unfortunately it has had the effect of making you petty and bitter. You wish you had his freedom, and you hate him for exactly what you blame him for. You hate him for being a man and able to do what you can never hope to do. You are a hypocrite, My Lady, considering yourself better than others simply because you had the good fortune to be born in this household. Please respect a more learned man, and if you find fault with not understanding the context of his works, then blame yourself for your intellectual shortfall."

"Am I interrupting?" Emma called out.

He turned away in disgust, not bothering to reply. He strode out of the room without a backward glance.

"Why did he turn on me like that?" Catherine asked, bewildered and hurt.

Emma avoided her eyes when she spoke, "He did not mean a word. He spoke in anger. Perhaps this author is a good friend of his that he highly respects. I know you better than anyone. You are not a hypocrite, nor do you believe you are better than others. Forget it, Cat, it would not do to dwell on it. You are entitled to your own opinion, and you did no wrong in airing it."

Catherine smiled to reassure her cousin, but her mind was in turmoil. She escaped to her room to think over his words. In spite of Emma's reassurance, she was aware that somewhere in his tirade had been a grain of truth.

She was honest enough to admit that she had been unfair in her scathing and very personal description of the author. She also admitted that she did feel a touch of jealousy every time she read accounts of travellers, who were almost always men.

Some sadistic part of her made her seek out such books over and over again. She would enjoy the detail and descriptions, yet the process of reading such material left her bittersweet.

She was disturbed to know that a man as good as a stranger had been able to list her faults so easily.

❖ ❖ ❖

That evening, Lord Raikes was overheard requesting his valet to bring him his travel diaries. Thereafter, he locked himself in his room for the night and did not come down for dinner.

Everyone felt his loss keenly. He was an outsider; hence, his presence had injected a vein of interest during meal times.

Catherine sat listlessly picking at her meal, her eyes bloodshot and her hair untamed. Emma looked as if someone had sucked all the energy out of her, while Prudence barely concealed her yawns.

The lovely dinner spread out in front of them looked morose as it cooled and congealed without being appreciated.

Catherine's eyes once more slid to Lord Raikes' empty seat and a soft sight escaped her.

The Duke thoughtfully noted his daughter's expression and declared an early night was in order.

❖ ❖ ❖

Emma entered her room that night with a heavy heart. Richard's smile froze as he noticed her expression.

"What is it?" he asked, pulling her towards the chair by the fire."

"Cat and Lord Raikes, they are constantly arguing. I think Cat hates him, and instead of leaving her alone he tries to rile her up all the more. I don't know him well enough to understand why he is doing this, but Catherine is behaving just as oddly. I have never seen her argue with anyone so passionately. She is normally demure and shy. I have rarely seen her lose her composure."

Richard curbed his smile. Instead, he took her hand and said softly, "They are attracted to each other. William understands this, but your cousin is confused. She is using anger as a means to keep her distance from the man, who she believes is your betrothed."

"No, I don't believe that. She hates him, and I have seen the dislike on her face every time she looks at him. I know my cousin, and you are wrong, Richard. It's all your friend's fault. I am sure he is teasing her mercilessly and deliberately annoying her. He may be attracted to her and trying to get her attention, but he is going about it the wrong way."

"Em, my friend is experienced and well-travelled. He has met all sorts of people in his life. He knows what he is doing. Don't worry about it. Your cousin will be fine, and I will warn William to curtail his behaviour in case others may notice and jump to conclusions. He will have all the time to woo her after our wedding." His tone gentled as he added, "Don't worry, Em, I don't like seeing you upset. I will talk to William and sort things out. Now, smile."

Emma glanced at Richard leaning next to her chair and offered a tremulous smile. He gently touched her cheek and pulled her off the seat into his arms.

Chapter 18

Lord Raikes had spent the previous evening and most of the night coming to the conclusion that he was a pompous idiot with a decided prejudice against women.

He had initially started writing to please himself, and using words he learnt on his travels had been a way for him to remember all he had seen. The indigenous words brought up the flavour of the country like nothing else did.

He had continued writing in a similar vein in spite of his publishers request to simplify his work for his readers. He wrote to reflect his intelligence rather than his desire to instruct or tell the world of the various curiosities he discovered.

He wanted to prove to that long forgotten love that he was better than anyone. He wanted her to regret letting him go, and over time, as her face faded from his memories, his methods became a habit.

As for Catherine, she had been unaware of the identity of the author. She did not know she had been insulting him every time she spoke. He could hardly blame her, for had it been another writer he would have laughed and mayhap joined in with his own scathing observations.

He had forgiven her, and he intended to make up for his earlier harsh comments.

He entered the morning room and found Catherine in the midst of unravelling a blue yarn.

He paused briefly to take a deep breath, and then composing his face into a mildly curious expression asked, "What are you knitting?"

Catherine eyed him silently, and then tilted her head in Emma's direction, who sat staring out of the window.

He ignored her hints and took a seat next to her.

"A sweater," she finally answered his question loudly, hoping her cousin would look up and join her fiancé.

Emma glanced up and smiled encouragingly in their direction, then went back to searching the landscape.

"Are you supposed to miss three stitches in a row?" he asked.

"Yes, it is part of a pattern," she lied.

"I see. What do you think she is trying to find?" he asked, nodding in Emma's direction.

"It's raining, I doubt she can see anything. Perhaps she is just thinking."

"What do you think requires such deep concentration?"

"Why don't you ask her, My Lord?"

"Oh, but I do not want to disturb her. She may be untangling some difficult problem. I may interfere in her train of thought."

"But you have no qualms in disturbing me?"

"No, since knitting cannot require a great deal of concentration."

"I could be solving some great, urgent problem while my hands remain occupied. Like you pointed out, I do not need to think to knit."

"True. So was something bothering you?"

"Pardon," she asked, confused, staring into his eyes.

He blinked, and a smile tugged at the corners of his lips.

"I asked if something was bothering you. What are you thinking of while you knit?"

"You," she replied, and then blushed in embarrassment as she realised what she had said. Her colour deepened as his smile grew.

"We are giving a party tonight, My Lord, in honour of your presence," Emma interrupted. She had noticed the scene and could sympathize with her cousin's dilemma.

"I look forward to it. Are many people expected?"

"Just a few families from the neighbourhood are invited. It won't be a fully-fledged ball, but we will have dancing after dinner. We have tried to keep the guest list relatively young."

"It will not be on par with what *you* are used to, My Lord, but we will try our best to amuse you," Catherine broke in.

"I am sure it will be delightful," he politely replied, immediately making her feel small for her slight jibe.

Emma had had enough of the tension between the two.

"Can you two get along for one day without sniping at each other? My Lord, stop seeking her out and disturbing her . . . and, Cat, you can say what you like with me in the room, but please do not behave like this in public. I will ignore it, but others will not."

She marched out of the room leaving them to sort out their differences. Richard had been right. She had carefully observed her cousin during the entire interaction and noted the blush. Her cousin had tensed the moment Lord Raikes had joined her. Her fingers trembled when she had tried to answer his questions.

The only reason Lord Raikes could possibly affect her cousin's composure to such an extent was if Catherine were attracted to him.

The misunderstandings between Catherine and Lord Raikes would not have arisen if circumstances had been different. She felt she was to blame, since the crux of the matter was the wager.

She wondered if the charade would ruin any chances of a romance blossoming between the two.

Everyone assumed Lord Raikes to be Richard; hence, she was worried Catherine would become a target for gossip if people noticed. Her attraction to Lord Raikes was clear as day, and people would assume that she was trying to ensnare an affianced man. Even Lord Raikes' behaviour would be noted and commented upon.

She finally concluded that she had been right in warning them. It had to be said, and she was the only one who could have said it.

Lord Raikes watched Emma leave, her words still ringing in his ears. He finally broke the silence and spoke,

"I think she is right. At least for tonight, let's call a truce. I do not want to give people any reason to gossip."

"Perhaps you should avoid me the entire evening that might be best." Her voice trembled as she spoke.

"Lady Arden?" He watched a tear fall and immediately pulled her into his arms, knitting needles and all.

She feebly protested, pushing against his chest. He murmured soothing nonsense until she gave up struggling. The moment her head settled on his chest a dam seemed to burst within her, and she wailed to her hearts content.

Lord Raikes was alarmed at the display of such excessive feminine emotion, though his alarm soon turned into contentment. He tightened his arms around her as he realised how right she felt in his arms.

"Hush, what is worrying you? I will stay as far away from you as you like, but please do not cry."

"You are not doing a very good job of staying away," she hiccupped and continued, "I cannot help fighting with you, and I truly am trying for Emmy's sake. She will marry you and go away. How will I visit her if you forbid my presence? I keep saying the wrong things and doing the wrong things around you, and I can't understand myself anymore. Yesterday you made it clear that you disliked me and that you hold a low opinion of my character, yet out of kindness and for Emmy's sake you tried to speak to me amiably. Whereas I cannot even manage to be polite in your presence . . . now even Emma has noticed. She will hate me for behaving like a child."

"I do not dislike you. On the contrary . . . " he stopped and clenched his fists in frustration. Then his face softened, and he lifted his hand to tenderly stroke her golden hair, "I promise by my honour, you will never be stopped from visiting Emma, however many times you wish, and for however long you want to visit her. I would never pose such unreasonable restrictions on my wife. She will have all the freedom she wants, including reading whatever inappropriate material she chooses."

Catherine laughed and then hiccupped. She rubbed her tear stained face against his shirt, and his muscles tensed. She felt the change in him and suddenly sat up.

"I made your shirt wet."

"It will dry," he replied gently.

She smiled hesitatingly, and his eyes darkened as he watched her lips turn up. That smile was his undoing, and the words tumbled out,

"Look, I am not what I seem to be. What I mean to say is that I am myself, but . . . "

"Are you alright, My Lord? You are not making any sense," Catherine asked confounded.

He groaned, "I am not alright, I am trying to explain . . . "

"What are you trying to explain?" Prudence called from the door.

Lord Raikes thanked God for her timely arrival. His friend would never forgive him for what he had been about to say and do.

He would have to keep his distance from Catherine from now on. The next time they were left alone he wasn't sure if he could stop himself from tasting her lips.

Chapter 19

"Emma, how did you manage to invite so many people and not one of them has met Richard?"

"Lord Raikes, credit me with some of the deviousness of the Earl. I only invited the ones that have not yet tasted the London season. Apart from that, none of them are the sorts that move in social circles belonging to your class. They live their life in this village, and the Duke encourages us to befriend them, as he does not abide by distinction. Unless it crosses lines of propriety, he believes in judging a man by his merit and not birth."

"That is noble of him. I have spent considerable time with your uncle since my arrival here, and I have learnt to respect him. Are you sure he is unaware of this charade?"

"Why, has he said anything?" she asked in alarm.

"Keep moving your feet, the dance is not over. No, he has not, but sometimes I wonder how we have managed to fool such an intelligent man. He hardly misses anything, and I find it hard to believe that he is not aware of everything that is going on in this house."

"Oh, he is growing old, and Richard's plan is brilliant. How can anyone fathom such an absurd situation? I am the only one who has met the Earl, and if I say you are Richard, then they have no reason to doubt my word. You worry too much, My Lord."

He stared down at her face thoughtfully. He was not so sure. Still, it was just another fortnight before this ridiculous plot was over.

"I wonder if we can delay this entire thing by another week?" he asked hopefully.

Emma stopped dancing and refused to budge.

"Whatever do you mean and why?"

"I need time to woo Catherine."

"You can't be serious? You are supposed to be my fiancé! We are meant to be madly in love. How can you make eyes at my cousin? What will people think? Besides, she believes you are in love with me and are to marry me. The more you pester her, the more you fall in her eyes. Even if she felt something for you, she would never admit it."

"I can't help the things I say to her, and the more I mean them, the angrier she gets. She thinks I am a cold, heartless man who is playing with her emotions, courting anything in skirts."

"Oh, you poor thing."

"I am glad you see my dilemma, while Richard thinks this whole situation is hilarious."

"Men can be so callous," she replied.

"Exactly!"

"Now, go dance with Prudence as I cannot stand her glaring a minute longer, while I go rescue my uncle from Mrs Barker."

"I thought you were sympathizing with me?"

"I was, but now duty calls. Oh, don't look so miserable. Once I am married, I will call Catherine over for a visit, and you can have three months of uninterrupted courtship."

"I am not going to wait an entire month to get her!"

"Oh, no, not you too. Why can't a man wait? First Richard and now you! Please do not plan some convoluted scheme to get my cousin. My nerves will not be able to handle another one of these situations."

"I am not waiting an entire month," he replied stubbornly to her departing back.

❖ ❖ ❖

"I need some fresh air, My Lord."

Lord Raikes stifled a sigh. Prudence had spent two whole dances clinging to his arm. He had hoped to be excused to ask someone else, but it seemed it was not to be.

"I will accompany you to the balcony if you wish?" he said, fervently hoping she didn't.

"Thank you, My Lord," Prudence replied, fluttering her lashes.

They strolled out through the doors, with Prudence having to bend slightly to avoid hitting her giant hairdo on the door frame. A little bit of hair from the top came off, and the curls scattered onto the floor. She did not notice, and he did not point it out.

She led him towards a dark corner, and he, guessing her intentions, started sweating profusely.

He was running through excuses in his mind when she leaned forward and pressed her full length against him.

He stared down at her pursed mouth and felt a distinct itch on his shoulder. Good lord! The girl was giving him hives, and he had to get away before it became worse.

Still struggling through his list of excuses he noticed Catherine gaping at them. She stood deeper in the shadows. He had not noticed her until his eyes had adjusted to the dark.

She stared at him in utter contempt and with a swish of her skirts walked away.

Snapped to his senses, he disengaged Prudence's arm and said firmly, "I am about to swoon. I need to go sit inside."

"Pardon, did I hear you say . . . that you are about to . . . ?"

"Swoon? Yes, that is exactly what I said. Now, please excuse me," he said forcefully, turning away and striding back indoors.

He caught up with Catherine as she tried to escape the room.

"We need to talk. I need to explain."

She stared at him accusingly, refusing to reply.

"Please," he begged softly.

She searched his eyes and then finally nodded.

He followed her into the dark morning room. She lit a candle and then turned to face him.

"I know how it looked, but trust me, she flung herself at me. It was not how it seemed," Lord Raikes explained.

"You must have read her intent, then why did you allow yourself to be in that position in the first place?" Catherine asked in disbelief.

"You know her. Nothing I said dissuaded her. I had to tell her that I was about to swoon before she let me go."

"Swoon, My Lord?" she asked, her lips twitching.

"Yes, dammit, are only women allowed to use that excuse?"

"No, but I expect men to come up with, well . . . manly excuses."

"Fine, I should have said something else, but that was the first thing that came to my head."

"I believe you, My Lord, and you need not worry, I won't tell Emma anything."

"I don't care what you tell her, just as long as you don't believe that . . ."

"You don't care about Emma?" she interrupted, shocked.

"No . . . yes . . . no . . . I mean I do not care what you tell Emma because . . . because she knows how Prudence has been behaving with me. She trusts me."

"Well, then she is a fool for trusting a man like you," she snapped.

"What," he asked, dangerously quiet, "kind of man do you think I am?"

"A flirt, a rake, a blackguard, and insensitive! You may feed me lines about not leading Prudence on, but I find it hard to believe that you would not take advantage of her if you had the chance. I have seen . . . seen the way you look at me, and it is not the way someone about to marry the love of his life would behave."

"In what way do I look at you?" he asked in the same controlled tone.

"Like you want to . . . " She blushed.

"Like I want to kiss you? Since I am a flirt and heartless and using Emma, then there is no harm in me looking at you as I please. Yes, I desire you. But trust me, I would not touch Prudence, even if she climbed naked into my bed."

The candle trembled in her hand, but she raised her chin defiantly, "I think I should tell Emma everything. I cannot keep your character hidden from her any longer. You are deceiving my cousin, and I have every right to . . . " Her words were cut short by a strangled oath emitted by him, and before she knew it, he had pulled her into his arms.

"You can tell her what you like, but I think I need to give you more to talk about than speculation and words."

"What . . . what do you m-mean?"

"This," he bit out, capturing her mouth with his own.

He kissed her roughly and passionately. Trying to show her, if not with words, then with his kiss how he felt about her.

Her inexperienced mind shattered under such an onslaught of senses. Unconsciously, her mouth softened beneath his and her body curved.

He changed the rhythm to a tender caress before he let her go.

She stood staring at him in a daze. She kept a hand on his shoulder to keep herself steady while he gently extracted the tilting candle from her hand.

He leaned over one last time to kiss her forehead, and then left her alone in the dark room.

❖ ❖ ❖

"Emmy?"

The Earl groaned as he dived under the bed, and Emma quickly smoothed her hair and straightened her nightgown.

"Cat?"

"Can I come in?"

Emma opened the door and allowed her cousin to enter her bedroom.

"You look flushed. Are you alright?" Catherine asked.

"Yes, I think I overdid the wine, but I am alright. Did you want something?" Emma said flustered.

"Can we talk? I could not sleep and saw the light below your door. I really need to speak to you."

Emma stared at the distress on her cousin's face and sighed. The Earl would have to stay under the bed for the time being.

"Sit, and tell me what is bothering you."

"Do you really love the Earl?"

The Earl, hiding under the bed, cocked his ears to hear the answer.

"Yes, I told you that already."

He grinned in delight, then frowned. He absently scratched an itch on his back as he thought about Emma's answer. Did she really love him? Then why had she not told him yet? He had tried asking her plenty of times, and surely she knew that. That blasted Duke always interrupted them at the wrong moment.

He decided to stay his happiness until she confessed it to him on her own. Finding out that your fiancée loves you while hiding under her bed was not very romantic.

Catherine's voice interrupted his thoughts.

"But the two of you behave more like friends than lovers. Forgive me for speaking like this, but I cannot understand it. To someone else it may seem natural, but I have known you for a long time. I feel like you are just pretending to care for him."

"What has brought this on? Did something happen tonight? You have already asked me these questions," Emma asked, concerned.

"Yes, well, I . . . I saw Prudence in the Earl's arms tonight."

The Earl grinned at that, filing away the information to use at an opportune moment. His smile froze as he noticed a spider skitter by.

He shoved his fist into his mouth and bit down hard to avoid squealing.

It would not do for Catherine to discover his identity like this. He squeezed his eyes shut, blocking the sight of the spider. Instead, he concentrated on Emma's voice as she said,

"I see . . . well, I know she has been eyeing him, and honestly I do not think he wants her in that way. She must have lured him,"

"That is what he said, but . . . " Catherine replied.

"Is there more?"

Catherine flushed in confusion. A kiss did not mean anything. Men, she had heard, did not need to love to desire. Her aunt had told her so plenty of times. He had kissed her, but what if he truly loved Emma, then she might be ruining her cousin's happiness. For a moment, her heart rebelled at the thought of Emma being his wife. She crushed the traitorous thought and decided to keep her silence.

"No, that's all."

"Well, then do not worry, Cat. I know the Earl, and Prudence is not a threat I take seriously."

But am I? Catherine wondered as she exited the room.

Chapter 20

Everyone was late for breakfast the next morning. Emma stifled her yawn. The gathering the night before and the Earl's visit had allowed her only a few hours of sleep, and the effects were now showing. She could barely keep her eyes open, and they were watering alarmingly. She blinked, trying to clear them.

Prudence walked into the room, and Emma was startled to see her looking worse than she felt.

"No, I don't want any breakfast," Prudence whined.

"But Pru, you need to keep your strength up," Mrs Barker urged her daughter.

"I feel horrible. I don't think I can swallow a bite. Not even a sip of tea."

Emma was concerned; Prudence never missed her breakfast, and the girl looked terribly ill. She was about to speak when the Duchess beat her to it.

"Try to nibble this piece of toast. You may leave it if you cannot have more than a bite. Trust me, you need to eat something. Just one bite to please me?" she coaxed.

Emma raised her brow at Catherine, wondering where the Duchess' maternal instincts were coming from. Her cousin looked just as surprised, and she shrugged in reply to Emma's silent query.

Prudence tried a few bites, and then managed to finish the entire slice of toast. She reached for another, and the Duchess poured her some weak tea.

"Now, drink up, and then off to bed with you."

Some of the colour was returning to her face, and Prudence quickly swallowed her tea and escaped to her room.

Emma got up as well, "I think I am coming down with whatever illness Prudence has picked up. I am going back to bed to sleep until dinner." She paused, and before leaving said to Catherine, "Take care of the Earl, will you? I cannot possibly keep my eyes open."

Catherine gaped at her departing cousin. The last thing she wanted was to entertain *that* man. She wanted to avoid him, especially after last night's kiss.

She had also wanted to use the excuse of feeling under the weather to hide in her room. She could hardly pretend now, as the other two had beaten her to it. Unlike Emma, she had not even had the foresight to throw in a few yawns during breakfast.

"You look pale, my dear. Perhaps something was wrong with the food yesterday. Would you like to rest as well?" Lady Babbage enquired.

She wanted to jump at the ready excuse, but perhaps it was better to get it over with as soon as possible. She would have to face him sometime, and better to see him alone first and get her emotions under control than make a spectacle of herself in front of everyone at dinner.

"No, I am truly fine, Aunt," she replied, pushing aside her chocolate. She left them alone to go hunting for the Earl. Now that she had decided to face him, there was no point in dawdling.

Lord Raikes, meanwhile, strolled out of the library, unaware that the object of his thoughts was looking for him in the garden. He went to the breakfast room to fortify himself with a cup of coffee. He sat chatting with Mr Barker and the Duchess while he wondered where the young ladies had disappeared to.

Catherine was quickly losing her nerve. She reluctantly took a turn outside, and then sighing with relief went back indoors. Perhaps the Earl was occupied with the Duke. Latching onto the excuse, she ran for the library. She, too, would hide out in her room until dinner, she decided. Why should she be the only one forced to entertain the man when she had got no more sleep than the other two? She would see him at dinner, and then take it from there.

She cautiously opened the door to the library and peeked inside. It was empty. Grinning at her foolishness, she strolled over to the books.

She chose five titles at random because she wasn't sure what she wanted to read. Balancing the books one on top of another, she nudged the door open with her hip and found the Earl staring down at her.

She dropped her books in confusion. This was the first time she had seen him since the kiss, and her addled brain vaguely registered him bending and picking up the novels.

"Here."

Absently she reached out for them, and her hands brushed against his. Neither of them wore gloves. She felt as if she had been burned, and she snatched her hands back.

The heavy books fell to the ground, one of them landing on her toe. She looked at him with eyes filled with pain and accusation.

He reached out for her, and Catherine panicked. She ducked under his arm and ran towards the stairs.

He leaned his head against the doorpost as he watched her departing back. A low growl of frustration escaped him.

❖ ❖ ❖

The dinner that night was subdued. Prudence picked at her meal and barely contributed to the conversation. Catherine's colour was high, though she managed to go through the entire meal without a single mishap. Emma was the only one in good spirits; her long nap had done her wonders.

The women retired to the salon soon after dessert, while the men passed the port.

Lord Raikes sat swirling the ruby liquid in his glass. The Duke had excused himself soon after the ladies departed, for he had an urgent business to see to. That left him alone with Mr Barker. He would have excused himself as well, for Mr Barker was dreadfully dull, but good manners forced him to sit until his glass was empty.

"Do you speculate, My Lord?" Mr Barker asked, eagerly leaning forward in his chair. It was clear the man had been waiting to catch Lord Raikes alone. He drummed the table with his fingertips as he continued, "I ask only because I have two excellent business opportunities. The Duke is very keen on one of them, and he as good as signed the document to invest in that scheme. Now, I would have kept this to myself, but you are, after all, going to be part of the family. So I am willing to share the details with you."

Lord Raikes frowned at the tapping finger. The man was sweating, he noted. His reasons for sharing a grand business opportunity with him just because he would be a part of the Duke's family soon sounded unconvincing.

Mr Barker was not the Duke's family, and even if he had been, he doubted the man felt any familial duties. He ignored his daughter and his wife and barely spoke to Emma. He kept his face expressionless as he nodded politely.

Mr Barker took this as an encouraging sign; his fingers drummed faster as he said,

"There is a gold mine in central Africa. We need finances to send experts to find the area and buy it from the current owner. You can imagine the returns on such an expedition."

"Why doesn't the current owner sell the gold himself? Why do you need experts to find the area? Is it lost?"

Mr Barker looked annoyed, and his fingers stilled. Lord Raikes heaved a silent sigh of relief as he waited for the reply.

"We know of it. I heard from a retired colonel of impeccable reputation that one such mine exists. Due to unfortunate circumstances some workers died in the blast the last time it was worked on. The locals believe it to be cursed; hence, they have neglected it and choose not to speak of it. I am sure the owner will be willing to sell it at a reasonable price."

Lord Raikes frowned. He did not believe for one moment the Duke would indulge in speculation. It was too risky, and too many people's livelihood depended on him.

This gold mine sounded vague, and he had the feeling Mr Barker was lying when he said the Duke was willing to invest in any such venture. Still, he could not outright deny any interest, and politeness bid him hear the man out.

"Africa is a dangerous country with an alien terrain. It would be hard to coerce the locals to speak to you, even if you do manage to communicate with them. The country is vast with a variety of languages, and finding a translator would be a task in itself." He continued in a kinder tone, "What about the other venture?"

Mr Barker brightened visibly as he spoke,

"I have a crew ready to go across to India and bring back a ship filled with exotic spices and silks."

"The risks seem high, do they not? I know the returns are good as I know of people who returned with enough wealth to live comfortably for years. But how will they reach their destination, with pirates plaguing the waters? An inexperienced crew would never be able to handle such a long and dangerous journey, even if they do manage to stay afloat through ocean storms."

"But the crew is experienced, My Lord. Why, they have made the trip five times in the last five years and have always been successful."

He frowned at the reply, disliking the man for outright lying to him. He spoke coldly now,

"If, as you say, they have travelled to India and been successful five times, then they must have amassed enough treasure to have no need for financial assistance. Why then are they asking for money?"

"You know how expensive England is getting, and these men only know sails and spars. They have squandered their money, and unlike us, they have no business head," Mr Barker replied comfortably.

"I find it hard to believe that within a year they spent an entire fortune that a ship filled with Indian spices brings. Why, it is as coveted as gems and jewels, and the earnings would have kept each crew member in comfort for a long time. I fear you have been deceived, Mr Barker, and I have my doubts if the Duke would invest in such a scheme. I implore you to stay away from such speculations. They are risky and the returns rare."

Mr Barker clenched his hands around the glass, and Lord Raikes hesitated momentarily. Yet the man had lied to him, and his conscience did not allow him to extend his assistance.

If Mr Barker had conducted himself well and treated his wife and daughter as a man should, then he would have, without a question, offered some financial aid to the man. But he had his doubts about what Mr Barker would do even if he did give him the money. The man was foolish, and he would probably throw the entire sum away in some ridiculous venture or a gambling hall.

He tossed his drink down and politely excused himself to join the woman in the other room.

Catherine spent the entire evening cleverly avoiding him. She sat talking to Lady Babbage until the older lady decided to retire for the night. She decided to follow her aunt's example and quickly made her excuses and departed for bed.

Lord Raikes lost interest in the company soon after her departure, and seeing his downcast mood, the others too became bored and turned in for the night.

❖ ❖ ❖

It was cold and muddy the next day. Catherine happily refused to accompany Emma on her walk.

Prudence still looked unwell, and finally it was just Lord Raikes,

Emma, and Lady Babbage, who chose to take a stroll in the garden.

The Earl watched Lady Babbage and Emma approach with Lord Raikes in tow. He quickly sat up so that the party had a clear view of him with his shears. They would not have a chance of a whispered conversation, as Lady Babbage seemed to be glued to Emma's side today. He nodded to them as they passed by.

His eyes followed Emma's departing back, but it was Lady Babbage who grabbed his attention by halting a few feet in front of him. He forced himself to focus on the old lady instead of Emma's appealing behind.

Lady Babbage was rummaging around in her sewing basket. She waited until Lord Raikes and Emma had walked a few feet away from where she stood, before turning her head and giving the Earl a piercing look. Satisfied that he was watching her intently, she dropped a piece of paper on the ground. She glanced back at him to ensure he had seen the paper. She surreptitiously inclined her head towards it, and then walked briskly to catch up with Emma.

She had just made his job easier by seeking him out it seemed. He got up as soon as the party turned the corner and snatched up the paper.

A single line was scrawled on it in an untidy, cramped script.

Weeping Willow Pond, Eight P.M

The Earl frowned and crumpled the note in his fist. He had wanted to find out what she required of him, but now that he had the chance he hesitated. Did he really want to enmesh himself in such a tangle? He already had his work cut out; did he truly wish to go courting something far more dangerous?

It was just the matter of speaking to the woman. He would listen to her, and he may be able to warn the Duke of some impending danger.

He did not have to heed her wishes, since she had no great hold over him. The worse she could do was to inform the Duke and his best friend. That was not a drastic situation. Besides, his curiosity was too great for him to let go of such an opportunity.

Chapter 21

Lord Raikes and Emma walked quickly, trying to outpace their chaperone. Lady Babbage strode just as fast, looking not the least bit out of breath.

They eyed the old woman irritably, increasing their speed. Their race was halted when they crossed the orangery.

"Isn't that the Duchess?" Lord Raikes inquired, staring at a figure standing in the distance.

"I wonder what she is doing here. She seems to be speaking to a man. Who is he do you think?" Emma asked.

"Perhaps a worker? She must deal with any number of people on the estate," he mused.

"No, she does not. Catherine is the one in charge, since her grace is normally indisposed," Lady Babbage remarked blandly.

"She is giving him something. I cannot see what it is . . . looks like a package of some sort," Emma said, shading her eyes to see against the glare of the sun.

"The Duke may have requested her assistance. Catherine may have been busy," he replied, unconcerned.

"I suppose so."

"Come, let us turn back," Lady Babbage said, pulling Emma's arm.

With a last look at the Duchess, she complied, and they turned back to the house.

❖ ❖ ❖

Emma returned to her room to change out of her muddy clothes. The entire beastly walk had been a waste of time.

Lady Babbage had not left her alone for even a minute, which had made it difficult for them to have a meaningful conversation.

Lord Raikes quickly changed with the help of his valet. He decided to go the morning room hoping to run into Catherine. He hated the way she had been avoiding him since he had kissed her.

He strode towards the room and opened the door to find the Duchess and Lady Babbage having a heated argument.

"I am warning you . . . " the Duchess snapped before she registered Lord Raikes' presence.

Lady Babbage pushed her chair back and walked out without a word of greeting. He stared at the Duchess in surprise, which quickly turned into alarm. Her face was almost white, and she was shaking with suppressed rage.

He rushed towards a pitcher lying on the side table and poured a glass of lemonade. He handed it to her and then knelt down to hold her hand, "Drink some, it will help."

She complied. Her trembling stopped, but her colour did not improve. He worriedly soothed her, all the while wondering if he should run for the Duke, when the door opened, and Catherine walked in.

She took in the scene of Lord Raikes stroking the beautiful Duchess' hand and jumped to the wrong conclusion. Her face flushed with anger and embarrassment. Her prejudiced mind barely registered her stepmother's pallor, her eyes full of accusations.

Lord Raikes guessed her thoughts and sighed. He spoke irritably, "Your mother is ill. Perhaps you can help her?"

Catherine looked back at her stepmother and noticed how pale she was. Contrite and concerned, she rushed to her side. Kneeling beside Lord Raikes, she asked, "What is it?"

"Nothing, it will pass. Don't worry, just call for some coffee. That should revive me." Her voice sounded stronger.

The coffee was called for, and she took her place next to her stepmother.

"Did you argue with Aunt?" Catherine inquired.

"How did you know?"

"I saw her face outside in the hallway. I tried to speak to her, but she brushed me aside."

"We just had a small disagreement," the Duchess replied weakly.

"Mother, you have never liked her. Why don't you say something to the Duke?"

The Duchess looked at her in surprise, "We had tried to keep it between ourselves. How did you guess?"

"You avoid her, and every time I walk into the room and the two of you are alone, I can feel the tension. You have lived with her for years yet never developed a bond. I know she is difficult, but I still wonder why you never hinted your concerns to the Duke?"

"We are both adults and can solve our own problems. You cannot get along with everyone, and living under the same roof is bound to bring out some differences. Besides, I did not think it was my place to request the Duke to move her someplace else. It is his decision as to who is a suitable chaperone for you. Even if I do not agree, I cannot do anything about it. She is, after all, my sister-in-law."

Catherine stayed silent, pondering her words.

"Are you happy with her being your chaperone?" Lord Raikes asked, turning to look at Catherine.

"I did not mind her a few years ago. She was kind, yet over the years, she has changed. She cares about me, but she refuses to venture out further than this house. She is barely civil to the young ladies in the village who I grew up with. She refuses to acknowledge anyone who is not high-born. My friends are respectable, and they feel insulted by her barely veiled disdain. She has succeeded in alienating me from everyone, and I wish I could have some other chaperone for a change."

He was surprised at the vehemence in her voice. He had failed to detect the depth of her bitterness. She maintained such a calm and civil demeanour in front of her aunt. He had noticed everyone giving into some irritation in her presence, including the Duke, but Catherine had always appeared to accept her chaperone without complaint.

The coffee arrived at that moment, and further talk was postponed. The Duchess seemed to have revived after her first cup.

Catherine set out to cheer her stepmother up, refusing to bring up the topic of Lady Babbage again.

Lord Raikes told them a few humorous stories of his childhood and soon the two women were laughing.

He was saying now, " . . . and then I sat on the horse without a stitch on. My father watched me from the window as I rode towards the stables in the dead of winter . . . "

"Oh, a moment, I have a message, can you hear it, My Lord," the Duchess interrupted.

He paused, taken aback by the sudden intervention. He politely left his story off and strained his ears. He could hear nothing.

"What am I supposed to be listening for?" he asked cautiously.

"My dear child, your departed mother wishes to speak to you."

The Earl's mother was dead, but his was very much alive. If he had ever felt that her grace was a genuine psychic, it was dispelled now.

"Hear her!" she suddenly screamed at him.

Alarmed, Lord Raikes pushed his chair back. Catherine started giggling. This was the first time he was being subjected to one of her stepmother's odd readings.

The Duchess banged her hands on the table rattling the spoons in the cups. She suddenly leapt up and pointed accusingly at him, "You have a message . . . hear her! She speaks to you from beyond the grave . . ."

Lord Raikes leaned back in his chair, casting beseeching glances towards Catherine, who ignored him.

The Duchess now came around the table, her eyes wild as she approached her prey.

"Listen!" she screamed as she stretched out her hand.

He panicked, leaning further back, until the chair tipped over and sent him sprawling to the ground.

He remained in the chair, his legs straight up and waving in the air. He had banged his head on the ground, though the thick carpet cushioned his fall.

The Duchess snapped out of her trance and rushed to him. Catherine came to his other side, both of them speaking at once.

"I am fine," he muttered.

"Your mother just wanted you to know that you have chosen a wonderful bride, and one day she will save you from hanging yourself from a chandelier. You should not contemplate such thoughts . . . Oh, my!" she trailed off, staring at something between his legs.

For the first time, he became aware of a cool breeze in the area where the legs of his breeches met. With growing horror, he realised that his crown jewels were hanging out in the open air, since his pants, along with his unmentionables, had ripped down the centre.

The Duchess was staring right at it with a look of pure admiration.

Catherine leaned over to see what was fascinating her stepmother so much when her eyes fell on the source. She clapped her hand to her mouth unable to look away.

He squeezed his eyes shut, aware of the spectacle he made. He could not believe that Catherine was seeing him in such an undignified position. His legs flapping in the air, his vulnerable nether regions exposed. On top of that, his brain seemed to defy his command to bring his legs back together.

The sound of the opening door snapped Catherine to her senses, and she jumped up and ran out of the room.

Lord Raikes peeked at the door to see who had arrived to witness his humiliation.

The Duke stood staring at the scene, and behind him entered Mrs Barker, Prudence, Mr Barker, and Emma. He groaned. It seemed everyone was to witness his embarrassment. He did the only thing he could. He closed his eyes and pretended to be knocked out.

"His chair tipped over. I think he hit his head. He was fine a moment ago, but he seems to have lost consciousness," said the Duchess worriedly.

"He needs to be taken to his room. I will call the doctor," the Duke replied. He turned to Pickering and issued orders.

Soon a few strange voices spoke above Lord Raikes. Help had arrived to carry him to his rooms. He had managed to pull his legs together when he had pretended to swoon. Now they hung limply to his side as he maintained the façade of being unconscious.

"Take his leg, Pickering, and be careful not to jar him. You, Davy, take his other leg, and you there, hold on to his shoulders. Now, on the count of three, lift him. One, two and . . . three!"

There was dead silence in the room for a minute. The two men had taken hold of a leg each of Lord Raikes and lifted him. The result was that his legs were split apart; hence, once more airing his unmentionables to the goggle-eyed spectators.

The Duke quickly blocked the view from the ladies, but it was too late. They had all got an eyeful.

"Err . . . Pickering . . . err . . . it would be better if you hold both his legs together, and Davy can hold him under the knees," the Duke muttered.

Lord Raikes was placed back on the ground, and this time his modesty was preserved as he was taken to his rooms.

"I did not get a good look," Prudence whispered to her mother.

"Magnificent," Mrs Barker replied, and then frowned. "What did you not get a look at?"

"His face, of course. Was he very white?" she invented quickly.

"No, he looked fine."

"Then what was . . . *magnificent*?" she asked her mother slyly.

"The Duke . . . and the way he took command, what else you silly girl?" replied Mrs Barker. After all, Prudence had learnt the art of deceiving from an old hand.

Chapter 22

The Earl had tears streaming down his face, "I cannot believe you actually searched me out to tell me this. It could not have been that bad. I am sure the main bits were hidden."

Lord Raikes smiled ruefully. He had come looking for the Earl as soon as he was pronounced healthy by the physician.

"Every little bit was waving out there. My pants were split neatly in the middle, and I felt decidedly chilled in that area."

The Earl, once again, dissolved into helpless laughter.

"Laugh at my expense, though Emma had a good look as well. You won't be pleased when she compares our assets and finds you wanting."

"I challenge you! Pull your pants down now, and we shall see who has the bigger . . . " the Earl spluttered to a halt.

A gasp had sounded behind them cutting the Earl short. They both whirled around to find a housemaid staring at them in shock.

"Err . . . it was not how it sounded. I know it sounded bad, but it is not as you think, Maria."

"Now I know why you ignored my advances, Shufflebottom. You should have told me that you liked the other sort. I wouldn't have wasted me time." She glared in annoyance and strode back indoors.

"Stop laughing. We are even now," the Earl grumbled, "I have an appointment with the blackmailer in ten minutes," he added.

"Shall I accompany you?" Lord Raikes asked, quickly sobering.

"No, I will tell you what occurs later. You should go back inside."

"Be careful."

"Of an old woman?" he scoffed, turning on his heels.

❖ ❖ ❖

The Earl found a branch to sit on and prepared to wait. It was almost half an hour past the appointed time when Lady Babbage arrived.

"I will get to the point. I will give you a day and one whole night to accomplish the task. If you fail, then tomorrow after dinner I will tell the Earl everything," Lady Babbage said as soon as she met him.

"What will you tell him?" the Earl asked.

"Why, that you are not who you seem and that you are having an affair with his fiancé. He will choose to, believe me, for young men in love are prone to be jealous and think the worst of women, no matter how innocent."

"I see. What do you want me to do?"

"Clean out the Duke's safe and go easy on Joe."

"Joe? The under-gardener?" he asked in surprise.

"Yes, and give him more free time. I need him."

"So, Joe works for you," he mused.

She did not reply.

"Why don't you ask Joe to steal the Duke's valuables?"

"He is more use to me than you are. If you get caught, then it's your word against mine. Who do you think the Duke will believe? As for Joe, I cannot afford to have him shipped off to the continent. I have bigger plans for him."

He realised that she had a bigger hold over Joe than over him. He would commit fouler deeds for her than he ever would. He could easily disappear, since she was not aware of his identity, but poor Joe was obviously trapped.

"I am afraid you will be disappointed. I am not going to clean out the Duke's safe. I would rather you tell the Earl whatever you wish. That seems to me the less dangerous option."

Her eyes flashed in anger. She had not expected to be thwarted.

"You will live if you are caught stealing, even if it is in jail. How do you plan to escape a duel with your life? The Earl will call you out."

"I am a good shot," was all he said.

"I will wait until tomorrow. Think it over. If you refuse, I will tell the Earl," she snapped.

He remained silent, and Lady Babbage, with a last uncertain look in his direction, walked away.

❖ ❖ ❖

The Earl met Lord Raikes in his room that night and brought

Emma along for the first time.

"I thought I should tell you both all that occurred this evening. I am becoming concerned with the situation. It is far worse than I had originally thought," he said, taking down a bottle of whiskey and pouring a generous amount into a glass.

Lord Raikes did not tease him for bringing Emma to his room late at night. The Earl looked worried, and his conclusions must have forced him to take her into confidence. He knew the Earl had tried to protect her all this time.

"Tell us what occurred," Lord Raikes said.

So he did and concluded with, " . . . what I cannot fathom is why the woman wants money. She is blackmailing Prudence that we know of. She may be blackmailing other members of the house that we are unaware of. She could have been doing this for years. She clearly has some hold over Joe. She has asked me, not for some paltry amount, but to empty the Duke's treasures. What does she need so much money for?"

"She has everything — a home, a carriage, silks, jewels, and anything else she may wish for. All she has to do is ask the Duke. Even if she does get all the blackmail money, where does she keep it, and what in the world does she do with it? She could hardly keep all that in her rooms here," Emma put in.

"She has another house?" Lord Raikes asked.

She shook her head, "No, you are aware of how little she does go out. She never spends a night outside the Duke's home. She does not seem too fond of extravagant things like diamonds. She wears the dullest things as if she is trying not to attract attention by being as plain as she can."

They sat in silence, each thinking their own thoughts.

Finally, the Earl spoke, "The reason I am worried is that her demand was preposterous. No wonder Prudence looked frightened. Had I truly been in the situation she had imagined me to be in, I would have been just as desperate. Perhaps I would have been forced to steal from the Duke. If I were caught, then I would have had no way to prove who the real culprit was. The Duke would not believe someone who was already indulging in deception."

"We have established the woman is evil, and we have no idea what her larger plan is or what she does with the money she extracts from people. Now what is concerning me is what to say to her tomorrow when she comes to me with your complaint. I can hardly pretend indifference to the fact that my fiancée has a lover hidden away on these grounds." Lord Raikes said.

"William, I have had time to think about it. This is what you should do. We have another week of this play acting left before I win this wager. You need to buy time. Tell her that you are worried and concerned by what she has to say. Yet you do not want to blame Emma outright without some proof. You want to catch them red-handed as it will allow no room for wriggling out. You want the man to suffer a harsh punishment. A man pretending to be older than his true age is not such a harsh crime. At best he could say he was desperate for a job, and hence created this farce. You can hardly throw him into jail for play acting," the Earl replied.

"I see, and then I should pretend to wait for Emma to slip up while she behaves like a devoted fiancé. It is, after all, only another week, and the argument to catch them in the act seems rational when you put it that way," Lord Raikes answered thoughtfully.

"I also think we need to keep an eye on things. If she is blackmailing any other person in this house, then I need to know about it. I am sure the Duke will listen to me, especially if I can produce some proof of the fact," Emma added.

The other two nodded solemnly.

"Now, I would like a glass of whiskey. It is a shame women are not allowed to taste such things. It looks delicious, and I always wanted to try it. I would also like . . . a cigar," she announced.

The Earl spluttered while Lord Raikes looked scandalized. They made hurried excuses of it being late and feeling sleepy. With exaggerated yawns, Emma found herself being pushed out into the hallway, with the door shut in her face.

Sighing in disappointment, she made her way back to her room.

❖ ❖ ❖

Lord Raikes pretended that he was unaware of the incident of the pants. It made it easier for him to get through the day. He ignored the blushing women when they turned his way, feigning ignorance.

Yet Catherine had been aware of his lucidity during the incident, and he was amused by her reaction every time they chanced to meet.

She was mortified and wondered when she would stop feeling embarrassed in his presence. Her face seemed to be constantly red since his arrival. One horrid incident had followed another from the day he had stepped into the house.

Things, instead of improving, had gone from bad to worse. This last incident had done her in. She lost her courage and could no longer meet his eyes.

Lord Raikes found her embarrassment entertaining. He did not care for other women's opinions and giggles, but Catherine's obvious discomfort amused him. He made it a point to search her out and speak to her, inwardly laughing at her attempts to fend him off and her comical stance every time she encountered him. She either stared at the ceiling or examined her toes, looking anywhere but in between.

His mood improved as the day went by, since all would be revealed within a few days, and he could openly court her.

He tried to make the best of their moments together, learning as much as he could about her interests. He read more into what she did not say than what she did.

Meanwhile, Emma behaved beautifully. It was easier for her, now that she knew him better, to play her part of the devoted fiancé. Whenever he entered the room, she fluttered her lashes and flirted with her fan for the benefit of the watching household.

❖ ❖ ❖

Lady Babbage approached Lord Raikes after dinner.

He carefully wiped all expression from his face as he engaged her in a conversation. He did not have to wait long before she asked him to join her on the balcony. Still pretending to be polite and unaware of her reasons, he escorted her outside.

"You seem fond of Emma," Lady Babbage said as soon as they were alone.

"Yes, I care about her a great deal," Lord Raikes replied.

"When do you plan to marry?"

"When the Duke gives us his blessing. I came here to convince him to shorten the time period of our engagement."

"I, for one, am glad he has given you so much time to think things over," she replied, her tone hinting at something sinister.

Lord Raikes played along as he answered, "Why would you wish for something so cruel? It cannot be kind to keep two lovers apart. We both come from the right backgrounds, and no one would object to our union."

"I think my brother is an intelligent man and he often has good reasons for the things he does."

Up until that point, Lord Raikes had not believed the woman would actually stoop to trying to destroy a man's life. He had no doubts now as to her allusions. She was angry with Richard for defying her in her request, and she wanted to bring him down rather than have her pride crushed.

He had hoped she would feel some compassion and give the Earl some warning to leave the grounds for good, instead of creating such a dangerous situation.

"I would like you to speak plainly," he said more crisply than he would have liked.

Lady Babbage paused at the tone, then misunderstanding the reason for his anger, said, "I know how the long engagement must irk you and of your impatience with the Duke. But let me assure you that had I not seen it with my own eyes, I would not have believed it . . . " She hesitated and then as if steeling herself said, "I thought it prudent to tell you before things are too late. You still have a chance, and I think you are a wonderful man and deserve better. Emma . . . she is having an affair."

"I don't believe it!" he exploded.

"She has him hidden away as the head gardener. I am sure you have seen her converse with him a few times. I have lived far longer than you, My Lord. I could tell something was not right the moment I met him. I discovered that he is far younger than he pretends to be. I am sure he is no older than you."

"Nonsense! Why, that man must be sixty, old enough to be Emma's father."

"He is a young man pretending to be a gardener."

"Are you sure?" he asked, injecting a hint of doubt in his voice.

"Yes, I confronted him, and he as good as told me that I was right. He pleaded his case with me. He does not have such a strong standing in society as you, My Lord, and he was sure his offer would be rejected. So he pretended to be the gardener to spend the last few months with Emma before she got married."

Lord Raikes wanted to laugh at the lies spilling out of the woman's mouth. He stared out into the darkness hoping his face was too shadowed to read.

"I know how this must distress you, but it is better you know now than when it is too late," she said.

"What do you plan to do?" she continued, wringing her hands

together.

"Call him out," he answered promptly.

"Is that necessary, My Lord?" She could not keep the eagerness completely out of her voice as she spoke.

"It is the matter of my honour."

"Would you not rethink, consider Emma?"

Very good acting, he silently applauded her. He might have believed the woman if he had not been apprised of the situation beforehand.

He controlled his grin as he curtly answered, "Emma . . . I do care about her, and I truly find it hard to believe she would deceive me so. I confess this whole thing sounds too fantastic. But if it is true, then by god I want the man to suffer." He wondered if he had overdone his despair. He peeked at Lady Babbage and saw her nodding satisfactorily. Pleased, he continued in the same tone, "But if I do approach him, then he would be sure to take the coward's way out and deny the entire thing. Therefore, I want to catch them red handed so there is no way left for him to escape."

"It won't be easy catching them. They are extremely clever," she said, getting annoyed.

"I am sure they will make mistakes. Letters and meetings are easy to ferret out. They are unaware that I know of their clandestine behaviour, so I have a fairly good chance."

"If you cannot get any proof, then what will you do, My Lord?" she asked irritably. She did not like waiting; anything could go wrong. The stupid gardener may decide to flee, and she had still not managed to uncover his identity.

"I won't wait for more than a week. If I can gather no proof, then I will simply confront him and be done with it."

A week, she mused, was not long. In the meantime, she could go to the gardener and say she had a change of heart, and she no longer intended to turn him in. Perhaps he would feel obliged to perform a few odd jobs for her.

"You know best, My Lord," she replied politely, ending the conversation.

Chapter 23

That night Emma and the Earl met Lord Raikes in his rooms. They laughed at his attempts to mimic the fierce tones of an enraged lover he had adopted during his encounter earlier.

The Earl got up and pulled Emma upright. He held her hands and spoke in mock serious tones, "My dear, I am a lowly gardener. How could you choose me over this man," he said, throwing Lord Raikes a disgusted look. "I cannot keep you in luxury the way he can. Noooo . . . let me go . . . marry him," he said dramatically, throwing his arm over his eyes.

Emma giggled, and Lord Raikes said in a bored voice, "You will not be rid of her so easily. She chose you, now you can keep her. Do not try and fend her off to me, though I agree I am richer, handsomer and own a larger house."

"I never said you were more handsome!" the Earl spoke in his normal voice.

Emma fell to her knees and proclaimed theatrically, partly to divert the two friends from arguing, "My Lord . . . I mean, my gardener, I would rather live with you in a tiny hut with roses and ivy than with this rich, very handsome man . . . who I admit is a little handsomer than you . . . ".

The Earl growled, and she quickly continued. "I," she said loudly, "would rather live with the man I love than . . . " She clapped her hand over her mouth as she realised what she had admitted. The Earl stilled and searched her eyes. The two seemed frozen in place.

Lord Raikes inwardly groaned. Did they have to declare their love in his rooms? He tiptoed towards the door and slipped out into the hallway.

"Em, did you mean it?"

"What?" she asked nervously.

"That you love me?"

"Do you?" she countered.

"Do you?" he shot back.

"You tell me first."

"Fine, we will be all night at this otherwise." He kneeled down to her level and took her hands.

"I do love you, Em," he said softly.

"I know," she grinned and seeing the look on his face quickly added, "I love you too, Richard."

"Why did you not tell me before if you knew how I felt?"

"I could hardly fail to notice it after you gave up your comforts to be near me. I thought it was understood and did not have to be stated."

"I needed to hear it," he admitted, gathering her close.

❖ ❖ ❖

Lord Raikes stamped his foot to ward of the cold. He had forgotten to bring his robe along, and he had no idea how long it would be before they recalled his existence.

He shifted uncomfortably, wondering what to do. He decided to take a walk to warm up. Seeing the look on Richard's face when Emma had admitted she loved him had made him feel incomplete. He longed for that love and surety of marriage.

He paused outside Catherine's door and stroked the wood. He knew he was in love with her. He could no longer deny it. He had fallen in love the first time he had set eyes on her . . . he frowned in thought . . . not love at first sight but surely at second sight, since originally he had mistaken her for a maid.

A few more days of waiting, he thought angrily. Yet he wondered if each day was adding to her hating him. The more she believed he was spoken for and flirting with her for the fun of it, the more she disliked him.

He had seen the growing confusion in her face. He knew she was torn between her undeniable attraction towards him and her brain that told her a rake like him deserved no respect, least of all her heart.

Perhaps it was time to let her in on the secret. He would speak to the Earl and convince him, he decided. She had to be told.

He did not want to wait for Emma to be settled and invite her cousin for his courtship. That could take months. But if she were told now, then he would have a few days to convince her that he was serious and never intended to have anyone but her.

He paused as his thoughts were interrupted. He looked around and found himself in an unfamiliar hallway. A door stood ajar, and Lady Babbage's voice floated out,

"Prudence, I am pleased you have found a way to pay me. I confess I am surprised that you managed to do so. I knew the Earl or even the Duke would not take you on as a mistress, so I wonder how you procured the sum."

"I have sold my mother's diamond necklace. The money will be here tomorrow. I sent a man to London today, and he should return by tomorrow evening. I hope this is the end of it."

"I did say this would be the last time that I asked you for anything. Yet, I cannot fail to point out that you will start showing soon. How are you meant to hide that fact from the world? You can keep my mouth closed, but others will not be so kind."

"I have a plan, and it is none of your concern, Lady Babbage."

"I see, well, I will leave a note in your work basket tomorrow night when everyone is abed to suggest a time and place. I will return the letters to you as well when I have the money," she said coldly.

"You are going to suffer for your deeds, mark my words."

"Is that a threat?"

"No, it's an observation. Now, goodnight."

Lord Raikes softly retraced his steps. He no longer waited for an invitation to enter his own room, but he did knock and wait for Emma to put herself straight before he entered.

"I am sorry to intrude on such an occasion, but I think you should hear this," Lord Raikes said the moment he was let in.

"That is why she has been ill!" Emma said shocked, after hearing the details.

"This is brilliant," the Earl said, and then at Emma's outraged look he hurriedly explained, "We need to get the note out of the basket. That is the proof we need. We will meet after everyone has gone to bed as usual, and then search for the note."

"She may carry her basket to her room," Emma pointed out.

"Not if she expects Lady Babbage to leave a note. Remember her walking in the corridors at night when we almost got caught? She may have a habit of doing that to leave messages for her victims. She will do that tomorrow, and Prudence will leave her basket somewhere other than her room," the Earl said confidently.

"Why does she not go to Prudence's room and inform her?" she asked.

"It would be too risky. She went today and already William overheard the conversation. She must be aware her visit to Prudence's room will be questioned, if by no one else then at least by Mrs Barker. Mrs Barker would not take kindly to her daughter being blackmailed. She took a chance today, but she is a careful woman. I doubt she will be so obvious again."

"But the note . . . how is that a safe method? What if someone else finds it?" Emma asked, puzzled.

"No one else but Prudence will have any reason to look in her own workbasket. Besides, Prudence will hardly air the letter, considering she is being blackmailed for a dark secret," the Earl explained patiently.

"Poor thing, I wonder what her plan is to hide her condition," Emma mused aloud.

"Escape to a remote village, I would think," Lord Raikes replied.

"We can do nothing more tonight. The only way we can help the girl is by bringing proof to the Duke," the Earl said soberly.

"Agreed. Now, I would like to sleep," Lord Raikes said, stifling a yawn.

The Earl and Emma wished him goodnight and departed. He did not sleep but lay awake a long time mulling over the day's happenings.

❖ ❖ ❖

The next morning the Duke took Mr Barker and Lord Raikes hunting. The women stayed behind to finish a leisurely breakfast.

Emma and Catherine had donned warmer pelisses and sat huddled by the fire.

"It looks as if the leaves are coated with caramel," said Catherine, glancing out of the window.

"That's a wonderful way of putting it. I can almost forgive the weather for turning," replied Emma.

"Prudence does not seem to be getting any better. She hardly eats anymore."

"I do feel sorry for her. Mrs Barker is almost rude to her daughter. She pushes her to enjoy herself, instead of calling for a doctor."

"Em, do you think I should ask the Duke to call for Dr Johnson anyway?"

"No!" Emma shrieked, and then continued in a calmer tone, "I am sure she is pining for London. It must be dull for her here after the excitement of the season. Besides, there are no eligible men here for her to set her cap on. She has even stopped flirting with the Earl."

"That may be it. Still, I worry about her. She is the youngest here, and even though she is annoying, I cannot ignore that misery in her eyes," Catherine said worriedly.

"Give it a few more days. If she does not improve, then I will mention it to the Duke," Emma replied, wondering how she could keep the physician from being called. No one could know that the girl was pregnant. It would ruin her.

They spent the morning pulling out shawls and warmer dresses from boxes and cupboards.

Emma kept a sharp eye on Lady Babbage, who looked as though she was suppressing her excitement. It could be the thought of obtaining a large sum from Prudence, but Emma had a feeling that it was something else.

That afternoon she came upon the Duke and Lady Babbage arguing outside the morning room. She heard her uncle issue a vague warning before he strode off angrily. Lady Babbage had a satisfied smirk on her face.

Emma curled her hands into a fist forcing her disgust deeper. She schooled her features as she joined the rest for tea.

The hunt had been successful. They would have a feast that night. The Duchess wanted to make an occasion of it. They all decided to dress up and invite some people from the village again.

The thought of entertainment brought some colour back into Prudence's cheeks, and Emma was glad for it. The invitations were sent out, and replies promptly arrived.

The Duke did not entertain much, and when he did, the villagers considered it a privilege to attend.

Catherine was on her way to give some clothes to the maid for ironing when Lord Raikes caught up with her. He pulled her into the empty music room, "I need to speak to you."

"I do not want to speak to you. Please let me go, My Lord. I have a number of things to attend to before the guests arrive," she replied coldly.

He let her go without another word.

❖ ❖ ❖

Emma insisted on taking her usual walk, promising to help Catherine with the details of the party later.

Catherine, after a brief argument with Emma, finally conceded defeat, and soon the two girls, along with Lord Raikes and Lady Babbage, went outside for a quick stroll in the garden.

Emma caught Catherine's eye meaningfully and discreetly tilted her head towards Lady Babbage.

Catherine blinked back twice in reply.

A few moments later Catherine let out a cry of anguish.

Emma paused and turned to eye her cousin.

Catherine winked, and Emma, grabbing Lord Raikes arm in a deathly grip, forced him to walk faster.

"I have a stone in my slipper, aunt," Catherine replied to Lady Babbage's query.

Lady Babbage was torn between staying with her beloved niece and chasing the rapidly departing couple. Her love for her niece won, and she decided to wait for Catherine, who seemed to be taking an awfully long time finding the stone in her shoe.

"When did you plan that?" Lord Raikes asked amused, after Emma explained to him that Catherine was simply hamming it.

"Just before we came out for a walk. I wanted a word with you. I heard Lady Babbage arguing with the Duke. I could not catch the words, but she is up to something, and I do not think it has anything to do with Prudence," Emma replied.

"Hmm, I will watch her tonight as well. We cannot do anything about any of her sinister plans, except find proof and present it to the Duke. We will have to steal that note somehow."

"Richard forgot to tell you that we will meet in your rooms at one in the morning," Emma said, glancing back to see how far Lady Babbage and her cousin were.

"What if the guests are still around?" Lord Raikes asked.

"No one stays past eleven when visiting the Duke unless it is a ball. The Duke likes to retire early, and everyone is aware of that."

"Your cousin is refusing to speak to me. Don't you think it's time we told her what's going on? I am sure she will agree to keep your secret for just a few more days."

"It is her father we are deceiving. I am not sure her loyalty will allow her to aid us in this charade."

"I think we should tell her," he said stubbornly.
Emma glanced at the resolute face in alarm.
"Speak to Richard tonight first," she pleaded.
"I am planning to."

❖ ❖ ❖

The evening was a success. They had all needed something to take their minds off their private troubles. The Duchess had become the life of the party, holding séances with some of the older ladies present.

Catherine avoided Lord Raikes, refusing to dance with him even once. Annoyed, he watched her laughing with some young man, whose name he could not recall.

Lady Babbage had given no hints of her plan. She had behaved as usual, hiding amongst the drapes in her dull brown dress. She had tried to encourage Lord Raikes to see Catherine as an alternative to Emma. This left him with mixed feelings.

The last of the guests departed, and everyone left for bed eagerly, each unaware of the numerous nightly activities planned.

Chapter 24

The Duke strode around the mansion fastening windows. Finally satisfied that the house was secure, he locked the front door and pocketed the key.

He glanced at Pickering who had been faithfully following him throughout the entire process. He gave a slight nod and Pickering, understanding the silent signal, left to see to his master's task.

The Duke then looked around one last time before making his way to his bedroom.

❖ ❖ ❖

The Earl sneaked into Emma's room that night and the two spent some time canoodling. They were soon interrupted by a knock on the door, and Lord Raikes' voice sounded outside.

The Earl cautiously let him enter.

Lord Raikes looked away from Emma's flushed face and spoke urgently, "Forgive me for entering your bed chamber, but I could not wait any longer. What if she falls asleep? She may already be asleep. But I really need to talk to her," Lord Raikes addressed the Earl in anguished tones.

"We are going hunting for the note, not talking to her," the Earl replied in confusion.

"Why would you talk to her?" Lord Raikes frowned.

"Why wouldn't I? Why should you?"

Emma giggled and interrupted, "Lord Raikes is talking about Catherine. Richard thinks you mean Lady Babbage."

Lord Raikes nodded absently. "I want to tell Catherine everything. It is not fair. You have Emma, and your game is almost over. Can I not tell her the truth?"

"He is right, Richard," Emma said. "She is a confused mess, and I do not like seeing her hurt. I hate lying to her even more. Now that she is involved, I want her to know the truth as soon as possible."

"Em! I will name my first child after you," Lord Raikes announced happily.

Emma grinned in pleasure, while Richard frowned, "But she will confess all to the Duke. I cannot allow you to do this just a few days before my win. All will be lost, after going through weeks of torture."

"I will convince her to remain silent," Lord Raikes promised rashly.

"I am not sure, William. Give me a day to think it over."

"No!" He exploded, "I am going to her now, darn it!"

❖ ❖ ❖

Catherine meanwhile was tossing and turning in her bed. She was burning with curiosity as to what the Earl had wanted from her. He had looked so tortured, and she felt terrible for behaving so badly with him.

Her embarrassment was no fault of his, yet she had perversely blamed him. He had not tried to do anything untoward since the kiss . . . other than being kind.

She spent a considerable amount of time analysing her behaviour. She ruthlessly acknowledged to herself that she had used her anger as a shield, to protect herself from the increasing attraction she felt towards him. She had lashed out at him to keep him at arm's length and protect her heart.

But her own vulnerability was no excuse for the way she had behaved with him. Her infatuation with him was not his fault.

The more she thought about her behaviour, the more restless she became. What if he wanted to confide in her about something to do with Emma? She was letting her cousin down because of her own selfish reasons.

❖ ❖ ❖

Lord Raikes entered his room in agitation. He missed the figure arranged seductively on his bed until a feminine cough alerted him.

He glanced up and saw Prudence lying under the covers. It was clear she was wearing not a stitch underneath.

He was frozen in shock, unable to move until a knock sounded behind him. He absently reached over to unlock the door and found Catherine standing nervously in front of him.

She avoided his eyes and instead looked straight towards the bed. She stilled and then said softly, "I am sorry to have disturbed you. It seems you are busy." With one last look at Prudence, she turned on her heel and fled.

He let out a whimper of frustration, startling Prudence. He took a deep breath to calm himself, then making up his mind, he picked up his robe from the chair and flung it in Prudence's general direction. He refused to speak to her or even look at her. He left her there without bothering to see if she departed his room.

He raced after Catherine and forced his way into her room when she tried to block him.

"We need to talk . . . NOW," He bit out.

Catherine took one look at his face and mutely agreed.

❖ ❖ ❖

Meanwhile, Emma and the Earl stole out of their room to search for Prudence's work basket. They tiptoed their way towards the main staircase when the Earl suddenly pushed Emma behind a suit of armour.

Emma's squeak of protest died in her throat when she heard footsteps close by. She held her breath and squeezed the Earl's hand.

Whoever it was seemed to be in a hurry and quickly passed by them.

Emma heaved a soft sigh of relief and peeked out. She noticed Mrs Barker's back disappearing into shadows.

They prudently kept silent, keeping their questions for later. They had taken a few steps down the staircase when another figure darted past them.

Mr Barker must have been behind them all the time. Yet, he pretended not to see them as he rushed away. A dying candle on the ledge had thrown enough light to identify him.

They stood frozen like petrified rabbits. Emma wanted to run back into her room and hide, but her compassion for Prudence won out in the end. They decided to proceed as planned.

Mr Barker may inform the Duke of what he had seen, but that issue had to be brushed aside for now. The note was more important. They quickly made their way into the salon. That was where they had last assembled, and it stood to reason that Prudence would leave her basket there.

"I cannot find it," Emma whispered in frustration.

"Perhaps the morning room?" the Earl whispered back.

"We might as well try all the rooms we can, Richard. I tried to keep an eye on her, but it was hard with so many people tonight . . ."

"Hush, did you hear that?" the Earl asked, placing a finger on her lips.

They stilled, straining their ears. At length, she shook her head and raised an eyebrow.

"Perhaps it was another mouse. I think we should not speak anymore. I feel as if the entire house is awake and prowling tonight," the Earl said quietly.

She nodded in agreement, and they continued their search. After searching for more than two hours, they gave up, and Emma returned to her room alone.

She undressed and got into bed, but the moment she closed her eyes a knock at her door had her sitting bolt upright.

"Richard, what's the matter, I thought you were returning to your room," Emma exclaimed, seeing the Earl back so soon.

"I tried, but the entrance to the servant room is locked. I don't understand it. It has never been locked before. I tried the front door and windows, and they are all bolted shut."

"I am sure Lord Raikes will let you sleep on the couch. You can slip out in the morning," she said nervously, shifting to block the Earl's view of her own bed.

"On the contrary, I think I need to sleep in a warm bed tonight. I am fed up of my hard mattress."

"Will he let you share his bed?"

"No, but you will," he replied smiling.

❖ ❖ ❖

Lord Raikes paced the room, and Catherine eyed him warily.

"I did not invite Prudence into my room. I found her there when I returned from Emma's room."

She gasped.

"No, no, you don't understand. I went to Emma's room to meet the Earl to ask him to allow me to tell you everything."

"You went to Emma's room to speak to the Earl. That is, you went to her room to speak to yourself? Then you returned to your room to find Prudence in such a state?" she asked sceptically.

"Look, it is hard for me to explain. It will take some time, so bear with me while I tell you from the beginning," Lord Raikes said agitatedly.

"I am listening, My Lord."

"I am not engaged to Emma."

"She called off the wedding! Finally, she has come to her senses."

"No, I mean the Earl is engaged to Emma, but I am not."

"I see, My Lord. I think . . . I think London has some fine doctors. This condition you have . . . is it from birth?" Catherine asked, nervously inching her way towards the door.

"What? . . . Oh, you think I am mad! On the contrary, I am as sane as you are. I am trying to tell you that I am not the Earl. I am not Richard Hamilton."

Catherine's eyes scrunched up in confusion. She searched his face and then asked, "Can you try and explain this any better?"

"Yes, I am trying. Look, I am not the Earl, I am the marquis's eldest son, William Raikes. I am Richard Hamilton's friend. We grew up together, and after my education was complete, I went travelling. I became an author and recently returned to England since my father is ill."

He glanced at her to see how she was taking it. She looked like she believed not a word.

He continued his narrative, explaining how the Earl had sent him a letter requesting him to join the farce, how over the coming days things had become convoluted as his interest in her increased.

"I wanted you to know because I could not bear another day of seeing you suffer under the misconception that I was a rake, playing with your feelings as well as Emma's. I implore you to believe me."

Catherine eyed him distrustfully. "So the Earl is the gardener, and you are his friend pretending to be the Earl? I find the whole thing too fantastical to believe. Is there any proof?"

"Emma will tell you that it is the truth."

"But why did she not tell me in the beginning?"

"She was afraid you may tell the Duke."

"I still might."

"Please, can you not keep it quiet for a few more days? If not for me then do it for Emma's sake. It is only a matter of another week. It is a harmless charade, and they mean no harm."

"I will think about it," she said, pulling her robe closer together. "Now it is late. Can you please return to your rooms?"

His heart felt lighter now that the entire secret was out. He stared at Catherine, who stood nervously shifting from foot to foot. Her wary eyes were shimmering blue, reminding him of a lake he used to visit with his father as a child.

He knew if he stayed a moment longer, he would kiss her.

They would both regret it later, he for rushing her and her for kissing him. He eyed her face framed by a riot of golden curls and decided to stay a moment longer.

She clutched the lapels of her robe tighter wondering why he wasn't leaving her room. She needed time to think, to come to terms with the fact that Lord Raikes was not Emma's fiancé. He was single, available and perfectly acceptable as a suitor.

More importantly, she was madly attracted to him.

She stared at his handsome face, and the emotion in his dark eyes arrested her.

The tick-tock of the clock on the mantelpiece faded, and her head swam as she unconsciously swayed towards him.

"Oh, I do not think so. I have a lot more to say," he finally answered her.

His husky voice seemed to break her trance.

"You do?" she squeaked, backing away towards the door.

"We still haven't discussed us."

"Us?" Her heart thundered in her ribs, and her eyes strayed to his lips.

He smiled in response and said, "You and me and what we are to do about this attraction we feel towards each other."

"You are mistaken, I feel no such thing," she said, panicking at the look in his eyes.

He put his hands up on the door to imprison her as he spoke, "Then I think it was time I proved it to you."

"What . . . what do you mean?" she asked breathlessly as the scent of him enveloped her, and her eyes fluttered close.

Instead of replying he bent down to kiss her.

He kissed her rhythmically and insistently, until she opened up under him. He groaned in satisfaction when her lips parted. He pulled her closer, running his hands through her silky hair. She moaned in response, and he abruptly stopped.

His breathing was ragged as he asked, "Do you deny the attraction?"

Her cheeks turned pink, and she nodded.

He grinned, pulling her flush against him.

She felt as if she were on fire. She arched closer, and her head tilted up, her lips parting for another kiss.

He touched her bottom lip with the tip of his tongue, tracing the outline, but refusing to kiss her.

She whimpered in frustration, and he whispered, "Admit it, Catherine, do you want me to kiss you?"

She swayed closer, her head feeling dizzy. He was no longer her cousin's fiancé; he had never been. She could kiss him, she had every right to kiss him and then . . . sanity intruded. She was in her bedroom with a man, wearing only her nightgown. She stared at him, growing frightened of the intensity in his face.

She pushed him away, and taken by surprise he fell back.

"Please leave," she whispered.

He looked at the fear in her face and cursed inwardly. He had not meant to scare her. She had to be wooed gently.

He gave her an apologetic smile as he left to return to his rooms.

Chapter 25

The Duke heard his valet murmuring above him. He dismissed it as a dream, but then he heard the louder voice of Pickering calling out to him.

He irritably opened his eyes, "What's the matter? It's early, and I have another hour of sleep left."

"Your Grace," Pickering spoke up from behind the valet, "it's an emergency."

The Duke glanced at the tensed faces in front of him and frowned. He had never before been woken up by any of his household staff. He sat up and waited for his valet to hand him the robe.

The valet stared at the Duke's outstretched hand in confusion.

Pickering leapt into action, handing him the robe instead, and then ran to fill the basin with cold water.

The Duke glanced at the trembling valet in concern. Something was very wrong.

"Pickering, get my clothes ready and send Davy down to the kitchens. He looks like he could do with a cup of tea," the Duke said, moving towards the basin and splashing his face with cold water.

He needed to keep calm and ensure that no one in the household panicked. He understood from Pickering's barely restrained agitation that the news was bad.

He gave himself a few selfish seconds to get his emotions under control. Catherine was fine, he chanted over and over. His daughter was safe.

He forcefully banished his morbid thoughts and finally turned to ask Pickering why he had been woken up at such an unearthly hour.

"Your Grace, the maid who attends to the fires in the morning always goes to Lady Babbage's room first, since she wakes up before anyone else in the house. A few minutes ago she entered the room as usual and found her dead," Pickering replied.

"Found who dead?" he asked, confused.

"Lady Babbage, sir."

His eyes snapped open. He stared at the anxious faces in front of him. For a moment, he thought it was a horrible joke, the next he dismissed the idea.

Perhaps the maid had been mistaken, and his sister had merely been taken ill.

"Come with me," he ordered, striding out in his robe.

He walked towards his sister's room, and with each step his heart steadied as it began to sink in that Catherine was fine.

He stopped outside the door and felt relieved. He could face anything, but if anything had happened to his daughter, he would have gone to pieces.

As for his sister . . . he paused to examine his feelings. After his wife's death, his biggest fear had been losing Catherine. He spent his days worrying about her welfare, whereas he had always assumed his sister would be alright.

His hand trembled as concern for his sister overwhelmed him. He steeled himself and knocked on the door. No one answered.

His trembling increased; his hand pushed the door, and it opened easily and silently on well-oiled hinges.

His eyes shot to the bed at the centre of the room.

Lady Babbage was lying on her front, deathly still. A large butcher's knife protruded out from the middle of her back.

He leaned against the doorpost in shock. His mind seemed to go numb, and then slowly his brain started taking in the details of the scene. He noticed the blood seeping through the white sheets and the brutal violence with which the knife was embedded in his sister's back.

He also realised that his grief would have to wait. Someone must have committed the murder, and that person was still in the house.

"Get everyone to assemble in the library within half an hour. I don't care if you have to throw buckets of water to wake them. Pickering, I need to see you before anyone else, so let someone else wake the household members. I want a report from you." The Duke mentioned two more names who he wanted to join the family.

Pickering looked taken aback at the request but left to do as he was bid.

The Duke changed quickly and had a brief conference with his butler.

Another half an hour had gone by, before a stranger was shown into the library. By the time he had finished briefing the newcomer, the household started entering the room. A few looked annoyed at being dragged out of bed at six in the morning whilst others looked curious and worried.

Mrs Barker was the first to arrive. She sat down nervously on one of the few chairs provided.

He assured her that he would announce everything once everyone was present.

Mr Barker came soon after and angrily demanded the reason for being unceremoniously woken up like this.

Catherine and Emma came running in before the Duke could finish soothing Mr Barker.

Prudence and Lord Raikes entered together. Prudence looked ill, while Lord Raikes was expressionless.

"Now you can tell us, we are all here," Mr Barker said irritably.

"The Duchess has not yet arrived, and I am expecting two more people to join us."

Everyone assumed one of the two to be Lady Babbage.

The Duchess strode in yawning, wearing a long white filmy robe. She had not bothered to change her night dress.

No one spared her a glance, each wondering what this great news was. From the solemn look on the Duke's face they knew it would not be pleasant.

They sent curious glances at the tall, reed-thin man standing beside the Duke. No one had seen him before. His hair was shocking white and his face heavily lined. His dark beetle eyes raked over all those present, dwelling long enough on each one to have them squirming uncomfortably.

They wondered what an outsider was doing in their midst, and they were further amazed to find the head gardener enter the room along with another strange man. Emma knew him to be the under-gardener, Joe.

The Duke stood up and came to stand in front of the desk. He looked around the room and said, "Now that everyone is present, I can begin."

"Father, Lady Babbage is not here yet," Catherine spoke up.

Mr Barker shot her annoyed look. He wanted to go back to bed.

"This is why I have called you here. It is about Lady Babbage. There is no easy way to say this, so I must simply say it. My sister . . . she died this morning."

A collective gasp went around the room.

The Duke watched the faces as they digested the news. He was unhappy to note that most looked relieved, Prudence being the most transparent.

"There is more, which is why I invited Mr Nutters to join me this morning. He arrived last night and was staying at the village inn. He had an appointment with me this afternoon, but the urgency and the nature of the situation forced me to request his presence early. He is a private detective in London," the Duke said, indicating the man standing to his right.

Mr Nutters bowed formally and smiled the smile of a shark baiting its prey.

This time the shock was slow in coming. It took them a moment to realise what the need for a detective was in such a situation.

"I see you have come to the obvious conclusion. She did not die a natural death but was brutally murdered."

"Is there no mistake, uncle?" Emma asked.

"No, she was stabbed," he said shortly.

Catherine burst into tears and turned to bury her face into Lord Raikes' shoulder. Apart from Lord Raikes, no one gave the gesture a second thought. Their minds were whirling as they tried to assimilate the facts.

"I am the Duke, and hence the magistrate as well in this surrounding area. It is up to me to find the culprit." His eyes turned cold as he scanned the faces in front of him.

He continued, "Unfortunately, the murderer is one of the people present in this room."

"But it could be the servants!" Mr Barker said angrily.

"No, it is not. The passage from the servants' room was locked last night on my behest. I also had a man placed among the servants, for a month ago something was stolen from my study. I wanted to make sure it did not happen again."

"You cannot seriously think one of us murdered her? You have your family present as well. You cannot think to blame them?" asked

Mr Barker.

"I am the law, and hence I have to be impartial and suspect *everyone*. I will not favour members of my family above any guests present."

He paused to let that sink in, and then continued, "Emma, please escort the women to the breakfast room. I would like to interview the Earl first," he said, looking at Lord Raikes, "and the head gardener. The rest of you will not be allowed to leave this house until the matter is resolved satisfactorily. Please wait until you are called."

Mr Barker started arguing again, but Prudence caught hold of her father's arm and dragged him out. The rest left quickly, each wanting some time to reflect.

Emma sent a last nervous glance at the head gardener before exiting the room.

The Duke waited until the door was closed before speaking. "Now, Mr Nutters will remain here during the questioning and aid me with his expertise. I hope the two of you have no objections to my asking a few crucial things?"

Richard and Lord Raikes shook their heads.

"Why don't you take a seat, Lord Hamilton?" the Duke asked, pulling out a piece of paper from his desk.

Lord Raikes moved to take a seat when the Duke looked up and said with a hint of a smile, "You, too . . . Lord Raikes."

The Earl glanced at him in shock, while Lord Raikes looked resigned as he sat.

"You knew? How?" The Earl asked.

"Please, give me an account of your nightly proceedings. After that, I will answer all your questions."

The Earl paused, wondering how he could admit that he had been in Emma's rooms. He decided to edit a great deal as he spoke, "We had reason to believe that Lady Babbage was blackmailing Prudence," he started cautiously. The Duke remained expressionless, so he continued, "Emma and I knew that your sister was planning to leave a note in Prudence's work basket to arrange a time and place for them to meet. We had planned to steal that note last night. We believed she would write enough in the note to implicate herself. We wanted to bring the proof to you before accusing her."

The Duke nodded and gestured for him to continue.

"We searched for it, but failed to locate it. Then I went to Lord

Raikes' room and fell asleep on the couch, since the door to the servant's room was locked. I woke when Pickering knocked on William's door. I hid in the closet to avoid being discovered and then snuck back into the kitchen. I was then informed that you had requested my presence in the library, so here I am."

The Duke looked thoughtful and said, "Can you tell me from the very beginning everything that happened which made you believe my sister was blackmailing Prudence?"

The Earl did not want to divulge Prudence's secret, but he knew he had no choice. This was a matter of murder and no longer time to play games. So he outlined the events that led up to their search.

"Thank you for your edited version of events. I know where you truly spent your night. Now, Lord Raikes, let us have your explanation for last night's activities."

"Your Grace, I am sure you are already aware of them, but I will tell you as truthfully as I can. I went to meet Emma and the Earl . . . in Emma's room," Lord Raikes threw an apologetic look at his friend as he said it. He knew the Duke was fully aware of their activities; hence, lying to him could not be a good idea. "I then begged them to allow me to tell Catherine everything due to my growing regard for her. I went back to my room to find Prudence lying in my bed. You can guess how she was dressed and why she was there. Before I could get over my shock, Catherine came to my door and misunderstood the situation. I then went to her room and explained everything as best as I could. I was thrown out within half an hour. I fell asleep soon after."

"Did either of you see anyone in the hallway?"

"Mr and Mrs Barker," the Earl said.

The Duke waited until Nutters had scratched that information down on paper.

"Did they see you or speak to you?"

"No, Emma saw Mrs Barker's departing back. She seemed to be in a hurry. We quickly moved towards the staircase when Mr Barker sped by us. He must have seen us, though he ignored our presence," the Earl replied.

The Duke thoughtfully tapped his lips with his fingers. He eyed the two men, debating on how best to handle the situation. He sighed. The murder was far more important than the indiscretions committed by the lovers. He finally contented himself with, "I have already sent for one special license this morning, and I will request for another as soon as possible. Both of you have compromised two young women. Hence, you will be married as soon as this is resolved. Lord Raikes, it is up to you to convince Catherine. It will not benefit me to lose my temper over such ungentlemanly acts, but I can only seek to improve the situation."

"So we are no longer suspects?" the Earl asked, grinning.

"I did not say that," he replied.

That wiped the smile off the Earl's face.

Lord Raikes spoke up hurriedly," Your Grace, I did not compromise your daughter. Surely, if no one is aware except for you, the matter of my being in her room can be overlooked. As for killing your sister, I assure you, I had no reason."

"Lord Raikes, I am aware you spent half an hour in my daughter's room alone and late at night. I have only your word that nothing untoward occurred. As for killing my sister, I cannot discount you, for I was unaware of your activities last night. I cannot know everything that goes on in my home at odd hours, though I am flattered you think so. Unfortunately, you have confided your indiscretion, and I cannot overlook it. I do appreciate your honesty in the matter, though. If you are proven innocent, then you will do the honourable thing and marry Catherine."

"How did you know my identity?" Lord Raikes asked, annoyed. Why had he not kept his mouth shut? He was in a pickle now, just when he had been making progress. Catherine would not be pleased with being thus engaged.

"I still have a lot of people to interview, so I will make this quick. Now, the first time I caught Emma with the gardener, I noticed something did not seem right about him. I kept a close eye on him, getting Pickering to act as my eyes and ears. He followed the Earl to the village one day and overheard a conversation with his valet . . . Burns, I believe his name is. He learnt of the charade you were playing and why. I then explained to Emma my reasons for asking you both to wait, hoping she would give up this foolishness. She remained stubborn, and I decided to invite you as a guest. She was indiscreet, and others had started noticing her odd infatuation with the gardener. I did not want things to get worse. I wanted you to live in the house where I could keep an eye on you and get to know you. You, instead of taking that chance, asked your friend here to impersonate your character."

The Earl looked sheepish while the Duke took a deep breath and continued,

"The two of you are the worst actors imaginable. Lord Raikes here gave himself away within five minutes of my meeting him. Had I not already been aware of the deception, I would have known through that first meeting. He pointed out a particular ornament I had brought back with me from Africa. He then told me in great detail how enchanting his trip had been. Everyone in London knows that the Earl has never travelled to Africa, since his parents died on their way there. I had investigated Lord Hamilton's interests as soon as I had heard of his engagement to Emma, as is my duty. And, Lord Raikes, that dye should have shown signs of fading by now. I am surprised my daughter, who I consider intelligent, never questioned that fact further."

"I have learnt my lesson. Living the life of a gardener for four weeks is a punishment in itself . . . isn't it?" the Earl asked hopefully.

The Duke eyed him blandly.

The Earl squirmed uncomfortably, and then dared another question, "Why didn't you stop the charade when you knew?" he said before quickly adding, "I truly have learnt my lesson."

The Duke smiled briefly before replying, "I am glad to hear it. As for letting you go on as is, credit me with a sense of humour. It was entertaining to see the three of you go to great lengths to try and hide the truth from me. It was, after all, a play conducted for my benefit. I did not have the heart to spoil your fun."

The interview was at an end. The two grown men stood up, nervously shuffling their feet. Feeling foolish, they avoided the Duke's eyes and making hasty bows scuttled towards the door.

The Earl and Lord Raikes left the room and the Duke to his thoughts. They strode miserably towards the breakfast room. Neither of them could contemplate the thought of going back to bed or eating a single bite.

The Earl was miserable since he had wasted four weeks of his life trying to fool the Duke. He could have had a warm bed within the first week of the charade.

Lord Raikes was sweating profusely. Not only was he a suspect in a murder, but he now had to inform Catherine of the Duke's decision. Catherine was engaged to him, and she had no blasted clue.

Good Lord! The entire thing was his bloody fault. He had tried to be noble and clever by being honest, but in truth, he had ended up blabbing like a nitwit. His fiancée would not be pleased.

Chapter 26

"Sir, you explained everything, except how you knew where the Earl was last night?" Nutters asked, once the Earl and his friend had departed.

"I had Pickering keep an eye on the house. I knew someone was planning to rob my safe. My mole in the kitchens informed me that Joe, the under-gardener who you saw present at the discussion this morning, was planning the theft. Pickering noticed the Earl going to Emma's room, and concerned for the young woman's virtue, he hung about until he saw them leave for their search. Unfortunately, he stuck to them the entire time they were hunting for that note and failed to see what else was going on in the house. Pickering might have mistakenly thought that the Earl was in on the robbery and convinced Emma to be his accomplice. The door was locked to the servant's entrance, so he felt no threat from that direction. He did not know of a greater criminal act being performed, so he wasted his time on the wrong people. It does give the Earl and Emma a strong alibi, even if they do not know it. I think we can safely cross them off the list."

"I see. I, too, can think of no motive for the Earl or even Lord Raikes. They were new to the household and would gain nothing from your sister's death. Still, we must reserve judgment until all the facts are before us," Nutter said.

"I agree. Now, I propose to call Prudence next. The girl looked unwell. She will need to retire to her rooms as soon as possible." The Duke rang for some weak tea and a pot of strong coffee, and then requested Prudence to come join them.

Prudence walked in nervously. She wore a demure pink gown this morning. She curtsied to the gentleman and sat down.

"I am sorry to have called you alone like this, my dear, but I wanted to speak to you without the presence of your parents," the Duke said kindly.

"That's all right, Your Grace."

"Now, can you tell me what you did last night after everyone retired to bed?"

"I went to my room and slept."

"Are you sure you did not visit my sister last night? You went straight to bed and stayed in your room all night? Please try and be honest with me. I promise not to judge you on any matter."

"I stayed in bed," she replied firmly.

"I see, now would you kindly explain how this," the Duke asked, pulling out a ruby brooch from his desk, "came to lie next to Lady Babbage? I found it this morning on her bed."

Prudence turned white, and then rushed to explain, "She liked the look of it. She saw me wear it, and I had let her borrow it sometime in the afternoon. I think she wanted to make a copy of the design."

"I also found these," the Duke said, pulling out a bunch of letters wrapped in blue ribbon. On top of the bunch lay a note to Lady Babbage from Prudence. "I am sure you know the contents of the letters, since they have been received by you. I also know that my sister must have found these letters and kept them. The letter on top tells its own story . . . that you, my dear, were being blackmailed."

Prudence started crying softly, "I did not kill her."

"I am sorry for distressing you. I assure you, nothing that has been discussed will go out of this room. I need your help, and if you did not kill her, then help me eliminate you as a suspect. Tell me what occurred last night?"

"I was to wait for a letter from Lady Babbage. She was going to put it in my work basket. I had sent a man to London to sell my mother's diamond necklace. I was hoping to exchange the money for the letters. That man returned sooner than I expected him, and he informed me that the diamonds were pastes. You can imagine how distressed I was. I deliberately took my basket with me to my room hoping that if Lady Babbage did not get a chance to leave the note, then I could buy more time. She already knew of my condition, and I am sure you know of it as well if you have read that letter. I did not know what to do, so I decided to go to the Earl's room and beg him for help." She refused to elaborate on what occurred in the room or her state of dress.

The Duke did not push her.

"Then," she continued after taking a sip of tea, "I returned to my room within a few minutes. I did not sleep nor did I venture out again. That, Your Grace, is the truth! I do not know why my brooch was lying by her. I had given it to her to buy time so that I could arrange for more money. She had seen me wearing it, and she asked me for it in return for keeping silent."

The Duke looked at the bitterness in her face. He knew he had got as much as possible out of her. It was a very likely possibility that she could have murdered the woman.

"What do you think?" he asked Nutters after she left.

"She is high on the list. She had a motive, she has no alibi, and the brooch was conveniently found next to the dead body," replied Nutters.

"But do you not think it is too pat? Imagine that the girl did kill her. She would have had to procure the butcher knife since young ladies do not make a habit of toting such things around. That means it was done in cold blood and planned. Why would she then leave an incriminating evidence like the letters or her brooch lying about for us to find?"

"Sir, the young lady is either telling the truth or is frightfully clever. The very fact that it is so obvious would make an intelligent man doubt her hand in this . . . and yet my experience has taught me that nine times out of ten the killer is almost always the obvious person."

The Duke nodded. He produced a bottle of brandy and asked, "Would you like a drink? Brandy, tea, or . . . ?"

"Coffee is fine, thank you. Who shall we call next?"

"Mrs Barker"

She arrived looking far more composed than her daughter.

The Duke took in her calm face and decided to be direct with her, "Was my sister blackmailing you?"

She was visibly shaken by the attack.

"I suppose you found some of my jewels?" she asked finally.

The Duke had not. He had merely guessed, so he said nothing in reply and simply waited for her to continue.

"Can I speak freely?" she asked, looking at Nutters.

"He has my complete confidence," the Duke replied promptly.

"Well, then, yes she was. She knew of the affair we . . . we had and threatened to tell my husband. Even though he turns a blind eye to my flirting, I was not sure how he would take it if he found out I had actually committed an indiscretion."

"I was not the only one she knew of?" he asked silkily.

She paused, weighing the words, and then nodded, "She knew of one other incident. She had also found a letter I had written to you in your possession. I do not know how she found out about the other thing."

"I see, and tell me why you were out of bed last night?"

"I went to speak to her. I wanted to beg her to leave me alone. My husband was getting suspicious and asking questions. I needed her to give me time. I knew once I returned to London I would find some way of paying her. But my husband refused to leave this place."

"Did you kill her?" he asked bluntly.

"No!"

He held her eyes for a long moment before allowing her to depart.

He turned to look at Nutters and caught the brief look of disapproval on his face.

"Don't judge me, Nutters. It happened right after I found out that my new wife was mad. I was in despair and turned to her for comfort. I was not thinking straight as you can imagine. I ended it as soon as I came to my senses. We had been lovers when I was much younger as well. I allow her to come here out of respect for those times."

"You need not explain your actions, Sir."

"I think I am still trying to come to terms with it," he replied, running his hands through his hair. "Let's not keep Mr Barker waiting any longer," he said, finally ringing the bell.

Nutters pulled out a fresh sheet of paper and dipped the quill in ink.

The Duke took a healthy drink from the bottle of brandy, letting the heat course through him. The alcohol did not give him comfort, and he pushed the bottle away, reaching for the coffee instead.

"I did not kill her. It is utterly ridiculous to suggest that I did," Mr Barker said as soon as he entered the room.

The Duke paused in the midst of pouring the coffee, and carefully set the pot down.

"No one is accusing you yet. Please take a seat. This is just routine. If you had nothing to do with it, then you will not mind answering a few of my questions," he said soothingly.

Mr Barker visibly thawed at the Duke's apologetic tone.

"No, I understand. I will do all I can to help. You may count me in. Women are such passionate creatures. We men should stick together."

"Are you suggesting that the murderer was a woman?"

"Women are emotional and jealous creatures. They often act irrationally. Why, half the murders in England are of wives poisoning their husbands or their lovers. I heard of a nurse who murdered her own children. Men are practical. They may kill to rob and feed the family, but what use is killing an old woman?"

Mr Barker seemed to become more vocal when he was nervous.

The Duke spoke mildly, "I know my sister did not have any affairs. Hence no one had a reason to be jealous. Besides, she was stabbed and not poisoned. That seems to me like a man's job. It is too violent a method for a woman."

"I see," Mr Barker said, becoming agitated once again.

"Now, please tell me why were you following your wife in the middle of the night?"

"I was not! I was in bed."

"Please, do away with deceit. This is a matter of murder being committed under my roof. Someone saw you."

"I suppose the gardener and Emma came clean," he said nastily.

"They had a good reason for being out of bed and together at that hour. Please answer my question," the Duke ordered sternly.

Mr Barker deflated at the Duke's tone and meekly replied, "I followed her to see where she was going. She has been acting odd this last one year, and when I heard the adjoining door open, I guessed she had left her bed. It was well past the hour for her maid to be in the room. It was my right to discover where she was going."

"Where did she go, and what did you see?"

"She went to your sister's room. She closed the door behind her. She was inside for about fifteen minutes before she went back to her own room. I was extremely agitated and guessed her reasons. I saw the gardener and Emma, but I did not think they would say anything about my being out of bed, since I doubt they would have wanted their own indiscretion to be known."

"I see. You returned straight to bed?"

"Yes"

"You knew your wife was being blackmailed, did you not?"

He looked furious as he glared at the Duke. The Duke passed him a glass of brandy, and he drank it in one go. He took a few moments to recover before he forced the words out, "It was a small thing that alerted me. My wife had asked me for money for household things. I remember her rattling off the list, and I had absently given her a few pounds. I did recall her saying she was going to get my favourite brand of tobacco. After a few days, I noticed my tin was empty, and for some reason that stuck with me. I should have assumed she had forgotten it, but I did not. I then started noticing that the meats in the house were leaner, and she wore paste more often than her real jewels. She was economizing everywhere. We are going through financial difficulties, but I bring in enough to provide for our basic needs. I was concerned. I soon realised that she was sending money regularly to Arden Estates, which is when I decided to come here and investigate. She was being blackmailed, and I wanted to find out by whom. I got my first clue last night, and this morning I find the woman dead."

"I thank you for divulging such personal and unpleasant facts. I am sure you understand that the circumstances warrant us to be honest, even if the truth is unpalatable. I will keep you informed, Barker, if I need anything else." The Duke dismissed him after thanking him for accommodating them.

Nutters waited for Mr Barker to exit the room and close the door before commenting, "If he had murdered the woman, he would have been more careful about being seen."

"True, the fact that he did not care if he were spotted proves his innocence more than anything else, although he had a strong motive. He is under financial constraints, and he would be furious to find out that whatever little he had left was being leached by an old woman. He would also be affected if whatever my sister used to blackmail his wife with was made public. No man wants the world to know that he has been cuckolded."

"He would turn his rage on his wife, not the blackmailer. Besides, he seems cowardly," Nutters pointed out.

The Duke nodded thoughtfully and said, "So the entire Barker family has a motive. They were all out of their beds when the deed was committed. Mrs Barker may have been the last person to see her alive. It is not looking good for the Barkers so far."

"No, Sir, this is getting more complex."

"You sound weak, Nutters. I think we should go have some breakfast. I do not have an appetite, but we need to rest a little and come back with a fresh mind."

"Very good, sir."

Chapter 27

"What is that gardener doing sitting with us at the table?" Mrs Barker demanded.

"That Gardener is Lord Hamilton, and he has every right to sit with us," Emma snapped.

"Then who is that?" the Duchess asked, staring at Lord Raikes.

"The gardener's friend, William Raikes, at your service," he replied, bowing in her general direction.

Mr Barker, Prudence, and Mrs Baker gaped at Lord Raikes.

"But . . . but . . . the gardener is a hundred, at least," Prudence stuttered.

Using his little finger, Richard wiped a bit of black coal from his teeth, and wiggling his fingers in front of Prudence's face, said, "It is a disguise, my dear."

"I do not know what is going on this house — robberies, murders, Earls pretending to be servants. I want to leave," Mrs Barker moaned.

"You forgot blackmail," Prudence muttered.

A deathly silence fell in the room. Everyone looked uncomfortable, and Prudence finally got up and left the room.

"I can't eat a bite," Catherine said, staring at her plate.

"Have some chocolate," Emma coaxed.

She pushed the offered cup away.

Lord Raikes took Catherine's hand and softly murmured in her ear.

She nodded distractedly and allowed him to lead her outside.

The others watched the couple depart, and for once no one dared to mention chaperones.

❖ ❖ ❖

"Lady Arden, I am sorry for your loss," Lord Raikes said as soon as they had escaped to the gardens and away from listening ears.

She nodded mutely.

"I know you had your differences, but you spent the most time with her. I can understand how hard this is for you."

"All I can think of," she replied, trembling with emotion, "is how I disliked her during those last few days of her life. I forgot about all her care and companionship simply because . . . because she didn't want me socialising. I wish I had been nicer to her or told her how much she meant to me."

He did not know how to reply or offer comfort. He simply walked in silence until they found a bench and sat down.

Lord Raikes waited until Catherine stopped weeping into her handkerchief. Once he was assured she had recovered her composure, he said, "I don't know if this is the right time to tell you, but I am afraid you will hate me more if you hear it from the Duke. I would like a chance to explain."

She looked at him blankly.

He bravely plodded on, "I am trying to search for the right words," he paused, and then said, "you are . . . umm . . . engaged, My Lady."

"Who is engaged?" she asked, confused.

"You are."

"Me? I don't understand. I am engaged, and I don't know it?"

"No, you see . . . you were engaged this morning."

"What do you mean by engaged? Am I engaged for some outing?"

"Err . . . you are betrothed to a man."

That snapped her out of her grief momentarily. She stared at him in astonishment.

"The Duke informed me of it this morning," he continued uncomfortably.

"He told you that I am engaged to a man? To whom?"

"Me," he replied sheepishly.

Her mouth dropped open in shock, and she leapt up and said, "Are you jesting, My Lord?"

He shook his head.

"Did you ask for my hand?"

"Err . . . not exactly . . . I was also informed that I am engaged to you."

"But how could he do this without consulting either of us?"

"That was my fault."

She glared at him, "I thought as much. Please explain clearly, My Lord, before I scream in frustration."

"Well, you see, the Duke, from the very beginning knew that I was not Richard."

She nodded in satisfaction, "I would have warned Emma had she taken me into confidence. Nothing escapes my father," she shot him a scathing look and continued, "but how did that translate into our engagement?"

"I told him that I was in your bedchamber last night."

"You did what!"

"He needed to know our whereabouts. I had to be honest. He is, after all, trying to discover the murderer," Lord Raikes pleaded.

She clenched her fists, desperately wanting to whack him on the head.

"It is a bit of a pickle," he muttered under his breath.

"Being engaged to me is a pickle?" she asked, offended.

"No, I want to marry you but not like this!"

"Humph, you do not look pleased with the news, and I assure you, neither am I. Do not worry, I will cry off and release you from this . . . this pickle, as you call it."

"No, Catherine, please, I am happy, but I was not sure of your feelings. I did not want to force this on you, and the Duke will not let you cry off. He has asked for a special license, and he wants to see us married as soon as possible. I wanted to woo you, as is your right."

"I did not give you leave to use my name, My Lord," she replied agitatedly.

"You are now my fiancé, soon to be my bride. I have every right to use your name, Catherine."

She glared at him in annoyance. She was confused, a multitude of feelings racing through her. Her grief and the news of her engagement . . . it was all too much to take in.

She searched his face, trying to find answers to her questions. Her gaze lingered on his deep blue eyes fringed with dark lashes and then travelled lower, stopping at his lips. She blushed and looked away.

He took her chin and forced her to meet his eyes.

"I am sorry that this happened. The murder, the sudden betrothal, the charade, but I am not sorry that I am attracted to you, care for you, or that inevitably we will be married, no matter what."

She couldn't help it. She smiled and he bent to kiss it away.

❖ ❖ ❖

The Duke picked at his breakfast, choosing to eat in the library rather than face the rest of the household. He was angry, since no one except his daughter had felt any grief at the senseless death of his sister. They were all pleased that she had been done away with.

Nutters was a coldly professional man and a stranger. He saw the whole thing as a job. No one could share in his grief. He did not think even his daughter felt the same despair as he did. He crumbled his toast and frowned unhappily.

His sister had been blackmailing a number of people, and he felt he was to blame. He had not provided enough for her, observed any tension in her, or noticed her need for money. She had chosen not to confide in him, which had led to her gruesome death.

Was he so intimidating, he wondered?

His reverie was broken an hour later when Nutters entered the room carrying a piece of paper. He had jotted down notes against each name.

The Duke picked up the sheet of paper and read the contents:

Emma
No motive
Her alibis are Pickering and the Earl
She was out of bed at the time of the murder

Lord Richard Hamilton
No motive
His alibis are Pickering and Emma
He was out of bed at the time of the murder

Lord William Raikes
No motive
Alibi is Catherine
Briefly out of bed at the time of the murder

Prudence Barker
Strong motive
No alibi
Out of bed at the time of the murder

Mrs Barker
Has a motive
Possibly last to see the victim alive

Was in the room of the victim around the time of the murder
Mr Barker
Has a motive
Out of bed at the time of the murder
No alibi

The Duke glanced through the notes, and his mouth pursed in distaste at the impersonal way Nutters had referred to his sister as a victim.

He roughly pushed the paper away and rang for Emma to join them.

"How is Catherine doing?" the Duke asked Emma as soon as she arrived.

"She is distressed, uncle, but that is to be expected."

"I understand you spent the night with the Earl."

Emma blushed, though did not seem surprised by the question. The Earl must have warned her.

"We did not kill her," she replied, ignoring his question.

"I know you disliked her and are confused as to why I kept her on as a chaperone to my daughter, when she was clearly unsuitable. I will tell you in the evening when we all assemble together, since I need to explain myself to everyone. I do not want to repeat myself."

Emma did not say anything, and he read her disapproval correctly.

"Emma, my daughter, is distressed, and my wife cannot cope in such circumstances. I am looking to you to help keep the peace in this house. I want you to handle the household. Can you do that for me?"

"I am at your disposal, Your Grace."

"I want you to do this as my niece, not because I, as a Duke, command you. I am requesting you, and you can refuse."

Emma softened her tone as she replied, "I know, I will do my best."

"Thank you," he said gratefully.

She smiled at him before she left.

"Not much to add here," Nutters commented.

"No, I know her well, and she is not someone who would stab someone in the back. If she did kill someone, it would be a knife in the stomach, with the person wide awake and aware of what was coming."

Nutters shivered uneasily and dipped his quill in the ink and waited for the next person to arrive.

"Catherine, I am sorry, I know how upset you are, but I want to get this over with as soon as possible," the Duke said, handing her a cup of hot sweet coffee.

"It's all right father. I . . . ," her mouth trembled, and she visibly forced herself to calm down before she continued, "I did not like her, but I never hated her enough to kill her."

"Yet you grieve?"

"I have spent a long time with her, more hours than with anyone else, and I know she genuinely cared for me. My feelings towards her have only changed recently, and part of it is because I wanted to be young and meet people my own age. I had always been happy with my books, until the last few years. I feel selfish now for disliking her for such a petty reason. She held my hand when I ailed and soothed me if I cried. She had been like a mother, I suppose. You may not like your mother, but you cannot help but love her either."

"Yet, for three years she kept you imprisoned within these walls. You knew part of the reason your season was delayed was because she had objected. She convinced me to keep you home. She alienated all your friends. In the end, she made sure that you had no one to turn to except her. It was a sort of obsessive, destructive love. The only one who firmly stuck by you was Emma. She refused to be cowed by my sister."

Catherine stared at her father's harsh face in shock. She had been unaware that he knew so much of what went on in her mind. With her shock fading swiftly, she became angry.

"Why did you let her stay in this house?" she demanded.

"I will tell you but not now. I want you to answer me first."

"Yes, I started hating her restrictions and yours, but that does not mean I will murder you tomorrow. It was your fault more than hers that I was in such a situation. You made her my chaperone, and you knew her best. If there is anyone to blame, then it is you," she sobbed.

"I agree," he said sadly. He came around and took her in his arms. "Hush now, I am sorry for being so harsh. I had to be sure. You may live with a person for years on end without knowing them. I had never conceived the notion that my sister would one day resort to blackmail. In anger, you spoke the truth, and that is all I wanted," he soothed.

"You believe me then, that I did not kill her?"

The Duke did not reply or meet her eyes.

She stared in disbelief at her father and slowly stood. She barely curtsied before walking out of the room. She kept her head high until she closed the door of the library.

The Duke pulled the sheet with suspects closer. He dipped his quill and wrote:

Catherine
She had a motive
Her alibi is Lord Raikes
Out of bed at the time of the murder.

"You trust Emma and not your own daughter?" Nutters enquired, baffled.

"Emma had to bear my sister's company only briefly during her visits. She thought of her as an odious woman, and her presence did not affect her life, whereas Catherine lived with her every single day and had more to gain from her death. She knew I would never let my sister go. She was, after all, part of the family."

Nutters rang for the Duchess instead of commenting any further.

The Duchess strolled in serenely and artfully arranged herself on the chair.

"Would you like some tea?" the Duke asked, buying time.

"I should be asking you if you would like tea. After all, that is my job," she said, amused.

Nutters mentally slotted the Duchess as insensitive.

The Duke, in turn, ignored her jesting mood. He spoke coldly, "Were you out of bed last night?"

"What time?" she asked, still smiling.

"After midnight."

"Yes, I was. I often walk around the house at night as you know. Last night was especially momentous, since I saw a strange vision of a man walking down the hallway. I followed him hoping to speak to him. He did not look like my father, so I think it was one of your ancestors visiting. Spirits have a way of knowing when a tragedy is about to strike a family. They must have come to give Esther support."

Nutters choked on his tea. He glanced in alarm at the Duke who ignored him.

"What did this man look like?"

"He was tall and blonde. I only saw his back, before he disappeared into the darkness."

"I see, did you have any reason to dislike Esther?"

"Yes, I never liked her. She was nosy and controlling. She always thought she was better than me, since I do not come from an aristocratic family. She never liked the fact that you married someone below your station. She would have preferred if you had kept me on as a mistress."

Nutters made another strangled sound.

"Are you about to die on us? Is the tea poisoned?" she enquired mildly, glancing at Nutters.

"The tea is fine," the Duke snapped.

"So, how did she die?" the Duchess asked, yawning.

"She was stabbed," he said shortly and then asked, "Did you do it?"

"I wouldn't ask how she died if I had done it, now would I? What sort of knife was it?"

"A butcher's knife," the Duke replied shortly.

"Ah, the spirits knew," the Duchess said triumphantly.

"What do you mean?" Nutters asked, sitting up.

"Why, I think that blonde vision was giving me a sign. I distinctly saw some sort of blade in his hand. The candle I held reflected off its surface. I thought it was a sword and the man from the dark ages. But now I see it was a warning for what was to come. I told you all a danger was coming, and no one believed me. They are often vague in their signs, and only when a thing comes to pass do you realise what they meant."

Nutters looked visibly excited at this news.

"Do you have anything else to add, anything further to tell me?" the Duke asked, ignoring Nutters.

"No"

"You may leave."

The Duchess floated out of the room. She still wore her white robe over her nightdress. She presumably wanted to return to bed.

"She saw the murderer!" Nutters exclaimed as soon as the door closed.

"It is possible," the Duke said thoughtfully.

"A tall blonde man . . . that fits only one person, and that is the Earl."

"You are wrong. It also fits the next person we are going to speak to, Joe the under-gardener," the Duke corrected.

"He is our man!"

"Let us first speak to him and then decide. Don't throw your list into the fire just yet, Nutters."

A handsome young man entered the room. His clothes were cheap, and mud stains splattered his shoes. Dark shadows stood stark in his white face. He stood nervously, shifting from one foot to the other. He clutched his hat in a deathly grip.

The Duke indicated the chair, and he hesitatingly did as he was bid. He sat.

"This is Mr Nutters, and he will be here during the entire conversation. You may speak freely in front of him."

Chapter 28

"Em, who do you suppose did it?" the Earl asked.

The two couples had met in the empty music room to go over the day's discoveries.

"I am not sure, though I think it could be . . . Prudence? She had the most to lose," Emma replied.

"Do you think she is capable of murder?" Catherine asked dubiously.

"I think anyone is capable of murder if cornered," Lord Raikes replied.

"Even the Duke," the Earl said, with a sideward glance at Catherine. When she didn't respond, he continued, "Emma heard him threatening Lady Babbage. We also know he was in some sort of difficulty, since we read his letter to Nutters. He had even stated in one of the letters that he was no longer sure what action he may take, since the situation was so dire," the Earl said.

"What about Mr Barker?" Lord Raikes broke in, catching sight of his fiancée's distressed face.

"He was scared of a mouse. I doubt he could murder anyone," Emma scoffed.

Lord Raikes leaned forward in his seat. "Mr Barker is in financial difficulty, and how can we be sure that Lady Babbage had nothing against him as well? He was deeply troubled and tried to involve me in some grand speculation. He was forced to appeal to an acquaintance for money. And he may have been aware of Prudence's situation. He would not want his daughter's name ruined either. He may not care about her, but he does care about his own reputation," He frowned thoughtfully, "The same holds true for Mrs Barker. It is more likely that she became aware of Prudence's condition."

"I can imagine Mrs Barker wielding a knife but not her daughter or even her husband," Catherine mused. "Did you notice that man . . . not Nutters, the other one? I think he was the under-gardener. I wonder why he was invited?"

The Earl proceeded to fill Catherine in. She had been unaware of her aunt's attempts to blackmail the Earl and all that Lady Babbage had revealed of her association with Joe. It had slipped everyone's mind due to the events of the day.

She heard him out in silence.

She finally said, "Joe must have done it. Why else would the Duke invite him to our conference this morning? He must have some suspicion. He was the only outsider apart from that London detective."

"You may have something there . . . I say, what about our old chap Pickering? He was in the house as well," the Earl said excitedly.

Emma smiled, "Just because he tailed you last night and blabbered to the Duke does not mean he is the culprit. You have not forgiven him for ferreting your secret out. And I doubt he did it. Lady Babbage was a highbrow. She never acknowledged anyone of the servant class. The only reason she noticed you, Richard, was because I showed an interest in you."

Lord Raikes nodded thoughtfully. "I agree. We cannot consider him seriously. That man spent the entire night chasing the two of you. He gave an accurate account of your activities. I doubt he would have provided you both with an alibi if he had committed the crime. He would have liked as many suspects as possible. He could have sneaked off once you went to Emma's room for the night, but he did not know if you would leave your room again. Besides, I also observed Lady Babbage's indifference to those lower in status."

"I disagree," Catherine said, turning to address Lord Raikes, "I admit I never saw her treat the servants badly, though she did ignore them. But how then do you account for the fact that she was blackmailing Joe? He was the under-gardener, after all."

They all fell silent at that.

The Earl fervently hoped it was Pickering. He wanted to believe it was him, yet something nagged him at the back of his mind. He had overlooked a crucial fact. He pushed his antipathy towards the butler aside and examined his thoughts impartially.

He spoke slowly, "Do you remember, Em, I told you that Joe had recently lost his finances and that circumstances had pushed him to become a gardener? I have dealt with him, though not at length, since the Duke employs forty other under-gardeners. I noticed him when I realised the man knew even less about gardening than I did. I felt sorry for the fellow and helped him out a bit. I had, at the time, mentioned to you that I did not believe he had always been a servant. What if Lady Babbage had been the reason he had lost all his wealth? He could have travelled to the estate to beg her to release him. She would have found his presence convenient for any of her nefarious plans."

"He sounds more and more like our man. He had been reduced to wearing rags and struggling for his livelihood. He is the strongest contender, along with Prudence. That also clears Pickering," Lord Raikes stated.

Everyone nodded in agreement.

Emma, seeing the dour faces around her, said, "Let us for a moment forget this awful discussion. It could have been anyone. No one liked Lady Babbage, and everyone had a reason to harm her. Instead, I want to ask my cousin if I should wish her happy. I see the two of you are no longer arguing. On the contrary, I believe he has caught your hand under the cushion. I saw you discreetly tugging away."

Catherine blushed and nodded her head.

Emma leaped up and hugged her.

The next few moments were spent joyously, the horror of the day pushed to the back of their minds but not forgotten.

❖ ❖ ❖

After dinner, everyone marched into the salon looking splenetic and gloomy. There was a brief flurry of skirts as the women raced to capture the most comfortable seats. The men politely resigned themselves to cold hardback chairs. Something told them it was going to be a long, long night.

The Duke strode in at last. He waited for the noise of tiny coughs, little sneezes and nervous mutterings to die down. When only the sound of crackling fire could be heard in the room, he began to speak. "I know you are full of questions. Uncomfortable questions." He ran a hand over his face, the shadows under his eyes stark against his pale skin. "To answer the most obvious one, I don't know who has committed the crime . . . yet. Although, certain facts are being investigated by Mr Nutters at this very moment. We will have a clearer picture tomorrow. My sister's body is being kept with the family doctor until the funeral arrangements are made."

"When can we go home?" Mrs Barker asked.

"You may leave after the investigations are completed. Now, I know some of you are wondering where your belongings are, things which Lady Babbage borrowed . . . They will be returned to their owners. I will need Catherine's help to identify all that did not belong to my sister."

Mrs Barker looked visibly pleased with this news. She even managed a smile.

The Duke walked over to the fireplace and warmed his hands. With his back to the party, he said, "I am surprised at all of you. None of you have dared to ask me if I killed my sister."

A few gasps sounded around the room.

The Earl and Emma exchanged guilty glances.

"It would be most convenient if I were the murderer. I would be investigating it and why would I implicate myself? She was blackmailing some of you, so it stands to reason that she might have been doing the same to me. After all, she knew me far longer and was aware of all my secrets."

He turned to face his audience, "However, I am not about to confess to any crime, since I did not kill her. As for her blackmailing me, she never dared. I was the only person in the world who could provide for her. She was a manipulative woman, but, nonetheless, clever. I am the Duke. If she did manage to find a way to ruin me, then her own comforts would be snatched away, as well. I was the reason that she had respect in society, access to many of her wealthy victims and the power to intimidate." He paused to let that sink in. "I would now like to tell you about Lady Esther Babbage, if you would humour me?"

Ears drooped, noses twitched and feet bounced restlessly, and, yet, no one dared to get up from their seats and leave.

The Duke sat back in the large, moss green, leather chair, took a healthy sip of whiskey and began the tale in a deep, haunting voice. "My sister, Lady Esther Babbage, was beautiful, frivolous . . . happy . . . . It all changed when she decided to elope with the vicar's son. The man she married, David Babbage, was a loathsome creature. Greedy, coarse and violent. It was clear he had only married her for her dowry. My father decided to provide Esther with a sum far less than what David expected in a hope that she would leave him."

"Did she leave him?" Mr Barker asked broodingly. He poured himself some more whiskey and swallowed half the contents in one big gulp.

The Duke shook his head. "David knew our father would eventually relent rather than see his beloved daughter suffer. Esther was only eighteen. Young, impressionable . . . silly. So he poisoned her mind against her friends and family. He isolated her until she believed with all her heart that no one loved her but him. He planned to bide his time, keep her by his side, waiting for the day when our father would break and give what was her due. But a man cannot hide his true nature for long. He gambled away the last of the paltry sum Esther had brought. Our father fell ill during that time, unaware of their rapidly deteriorating financial state."

"You could have helped her," Catherine said.

The Duke shook his head. "He was the Duke, head of the family. How could I go against his wishes? We believed that she would write to us if things became unbearable. She didn't. Pride held her back. She refused to grovel before a family she believed had abandoned her. Years slipped by, David grew violent in his demands for money. Tried to force Esther to go to our father to beg and plead her pathetic case . . . She could have left then. She had grown to hate her husband with a passion. The only reason she stayed on was for the sake of her son."

"Son?" Catherine and Emma exclaimed.

"But she never spoke of any children," Catherine frowned.

The Duke waited until the excited voices died down. "Her husband died in a senseless brawl one night. Her son was now grown up. Unfortunately, he turned out to be no better than his father. He disliked his mother and made demands similar to those that his father had made. The difference was that she loved him like she had never loved her husband. But pride still gripped her. When threats and pleas to return to the Arden Estates failed to move his mother, the boy ran away to London and she lost all trace of him. Meanwhile, my father died and I succeeded him as the Duke. My first job was to find my sister and convince her to return with me."

"What made her come back with you?" Mr Barker asked. His mood seemed to have improved. His cheeks had turned a lovely shade of pink. "Spanked the pride out of her did you?"

Catherine sucked in a horrified breath, Emma giggled, and Mrs Barker leaned over and plucked the glass of whiskey out of her husband's hand.

The Duke ignored the interruption and continued, "My wife had just died and I had a young daughter. I appealed to Esther to come and take care of my child. Esther's pride was mollified when she realised she would not be a charity case but was truly needed. She had always been fond of children and took to Catherine immediately."

"Why? I thought you were an intelligent man," Mr Barker boomed across the room at him. "How could you allow your child to be brought up by that nefarious creature? That saucy, mouldy mushroom —

"Hush, she is dead," Mrs Barker whacked him on the head.

The Duke smiled wryly, "I saw what I wanted to see. I failed to notice the changes in my sister. Failed to conceive the depth of cruelty she may have suffered. Her experiences had hardened her, made her shrewder, sharper like a well-wrought knife. The only thing I asked of her was to treat my daughter fairly. She managed her side of the bargain reasonably well, until her son came back into her life."

"He is still alive? But we have never seen him," Catherine exclaimed in shock.

"You all have seen him. Let me continue."

Catherine nodded.

The Duke stared at the fire, watching a log break in the heat. "Her son was greatly in debt and fleeing from the law. He found out that his mother was back in a comfortable position and he decided to ask her for money. He sent her a note and she panicked. She knew I would never allow that kind of man to be under the same roof as my daughter. She met her son secretly and he made her promise that she would give him something in return. She had missed him when he had abandoned her and she was afraid of losing him once again. She relented and gave him all the jewels she had, with which he paid off some of his debts. He then returned for more. She asked me for it and I gave it to her with a warning that no more would be forthcoming. I knew that boy would leech his mother dry if he could. The only way to stop him would have been to refuse to pay him and instead force him to live an honest man's life. You can guess what happened next. He kept coming and Esther was forced to find other means of payment. She happened upon a secret and found a perfect source of income through blackmail. A month back, the boy returned, and Esther had to stoop to robbing me to pay her son off. She was willing to do anything to keep him in her life."

The Duke paused and the sudden silence seemed deafening. He let the silence linger. It allowed the echo of his words to wrap around his listeners and sink in.

The ticking of the grandfather clock and the crackling and spitting flames in the fireplace was the only sound to be heard in the stillness.

No one dared to interrupt the silence until the Duke spoke again. "I confess I did not know or even conceive that she had resorted to such means. Her behaviour was so correct at all times. I knew she genuinely loved my daughter, and I felt guilty for keeping her away from her son. Because of that guilt, I allowed her to dictate my daughter's life and occasionally override my own wishes regarding her upbringing. I wanted to give her a child in return for taking one away from her. I let her isolate my only child, the same way she had been isolated by her husband. I think, since she had been bullied for so long, she wanted to be the one in command and keep others dependent on her. She became the bully, and I failed to see it. She used emotions like guilt, jealousy, and love against all of us to force us to do what she desired. I blame myself for most of it. I should have taken the boy in hand instead of pushing him away. She knew me best, and hence all my faults were easy to manipulate. She did not need to blackmail me to make me do as she wished. I compromised my daughter's happiness, after all."

Catherine got up and approached her father. She set his glass away and embraced him.

He hid his face in her shoulder. His eyes turned wet.

She said gently, "I was happy except for the last three years. I am sorry I was angry. It was not your fault. If anything, it was aunt's fault. Her methods can have no reasonable excuse. Everyone suffers, but not everyone chooses to take such a malicious path."

The Duke felt as if a great weight had lifted off his shoulders. He pushed her away to look into her face, "You have grown wise, child."

She kissed the top of his head as she answered,

"I had the best teacher in you."

Chapter 29

After a sleepless night, the household woke up with a feeling of dread. The Duke would reveal the murderer today.

Everyone had broken into little groups and found separate corners to spend their morning. The Barker family sat huddled together in the breakfast room. Emma and the Earl had left to stroll in the gardens. The Duke was locked in his study with Nutters, while Lady Arden was still in bed.

"Have you truly forgiven your father?" Lord Raikes asked Catherine.

Catherine's eyes skittered around the library. Only after ascertaining that they were alone did she reply, "I was miserable having my aunt as my chaperone. Yet, all through those years I was convinced my father was doing what he thought was best for me. I believed that with time I would come to understand his reasoning. I-I sympathise with his situation. It is difficult to see him as vulnerable." She paused and then added on a more forceful note, "but I am also angry, for how could he make such a mistake? I thought he was perfect and could do no wrong."

"I think he is a better man than most of us. It is not easy to concede one's faults, and for such a proud man, it is harder still. I think he did it for you," Lord Raikes said gently.

"I know he did it for me. I truly appreciate that, but words cannot heal old sores, only time can do that."

"Don't let it fester into hatred. He only wants what is best for you," he cautioned.

"He thinks I may have murdered my aunt. I cannot forgive that so easily. I wish the killer is caught soon. This situation is making me suspicious of everyone. I cannot help staring around the room and wondering who murdered her. I cannot dismiss anyone, not even

Emma. I had even suspected my father. I know that's hypocritical. He has every right to suspect me if I feel the same way. My brain tells me that he is not wrong in doing so, yet my heart rebels at the thought."

"Do you think I did it?" Lord Raikes asked, searching her face.

She glanced up at him and did not answer.

He sighed. He could hardly expect to be discounted as the murderer if she was suspicious of even the Duke. This was a new tangle that interfered with their romance and he, too, could not wait for the killer to be caught.

His beautiful fiancée could hardly fall in love with a man she suspected of being a murderer.

❖ ❖ ❖

That evening the Duke asked them to assemble in the library once more. Nutters was present armed with his quill and paper.

"Good evening. Some new evidence have come to light, and I wanted to share it with you," the Duke announced.

Everyone faced the Duke, controlling their nervous fidgeting.

"I do not have the luxury to discount anyone, not even my own family members. Being a Duke has its advantages, yet at times like this, I wish I did not hold this title. I am torn between duty towards my family and my responsibilities. Please forgive me for what is about to follow. I am also bound to avenge my sister's death, and that is why I will speak to you as a Duke and not as a friend, husband, uncle, or father." He gazed around the room, his eyes resigned.

Not a squeak of protest was heard. The Duke was not asking them but informing them.

The Duke continued after a moment, "I think it is only fair to all present that I first start with my daughter. Catherine had spent the most time with my sister, who was, as we all know, a difficult person. It was because of her that my daughter was literally a prisoner in her own home. She was alienated from her friends and from her family. She came to hate her aunt with a passion."

He put up his hand to stall Lord Raikes, who had risen from his seat to argue. "I know what you are going to tell me, that she loved her as well, like no one else present in this room did. Lord Raikes, a person commits a crime out of an intense emotion. It is easier for love to turn into hatred than mere dislike. She loved the memory of her aunt as she had been during her childhood, allowing her to escape to the library when she pleased, encouraging her shyness, and soothing her tears. When Catherine grew up, she slowly understood the negative aspects of her aunt's attitude and how it was affecting her life and personality. She is an intelligent girl, and she slowly realised that she could never hope to grow as a person with her aunt acting as her guardian. She needed to break free of her influence and for once breathe. She had been suffocating. I would never let my sister go. How could I be expected to choose between a daughter and a sister? So she had the motive to kill. She runs the household, hence her procuring a butcher's knife was not a problem. Finally, she does not have an alibi, and her room is closest to my sister's."

Catherine had turned white. Lord Raikes held her hand and glared at the Duke and asked, "How can you accuse your own daughter?"

"I am merely stating facts," the Duke replied dispassionately.

"Are you saying your daughter is the murderer?" Mr Barker enquired.

"No, I am not confirming who the murderer is . . . yet. I am simply telling you how she had the means and the motive. I will now come to you, Lord Raikes," he said, turning to face the furious man, "you are in love with my daughter."

A few gasps sounded around the room. Not everyone had been aware of this new development.

Catherine quickly glanced at Lord Raikes and was surprised to find that he did not deny it.

The Duke ignored the murmurs. Instead, he continued eyeing Lord Raikes as he spoke, "Now, why would you have any reason to murder my sister? You had the means and no alibi. You were awake at the time of the murder by your own admission, but what could be the reason? I think you were afraid Lady Babbage would never let Catherine go. You saw the depth of her possessiveness."

"I am sorry to spoil your theory midway, Your Grace," Lord Raikes interrupted, "Lady Babbage had encouraged me to pursue Catherine and forget Emma."

"We have only your word to prove that, but let us assume you are speaking the truth. She encouraged you in your efforts to woo Catherine. Let us even assume she allowed you two to marry. Tell me, Lord Raikes, do you think a change in marital status would have affected her hold on my daughter? She had years to work on her charge. She had ample time to mould her into a perfect, biddable girl who did as she was told. You saw how submissive my daughter was, and you were not sure if you could ever free Catherine from my sister's clutches. You are also a passionate man, and I think your love is all consuming. You cannot bear to share the one you love with anyone else. You love her enough to want her to grow into her own person. The only way she could be a confident and secure young woman was if her aunt were removed from the scene."

"It sounds a bit improbable, Sir," the Earl commented.

"I am surprised to hear you say that. You know him best and are surely aware of his past. He did not return to England for ten years because his first love refused to have him. Can you fathom what a man of such deep emotions is capable of? He fell in love once more, and this time he intends to have his beloved. He did not mention his indiscretion to me yesterday out of any sense of honesty or belief in my omniscience. He told me what occurred truthfully because he knew the result. I would have no choice but to get the two of them wed as soon as I possibly could."

Lord Raikes stayed silent, neither confirming nor denying anything.

The Duke gazed at his future son-in-law and smiled, "He will not proclaim his innocence until he is sure that Catherine is safe from the gallows. Would anyone like tea or some wine?"

No one bothered to reply.

The Duke shrugged and refilled his own glass; taking a sip he continued, "Emma now has two people who can vouch for her actions on that fated night. Though, she did have a motive . . . her concern for her cousin. She loves her as a sister. No one else knew the depth of Lady Babbage's effect on Catherine better than Emma. She could see how her cousin's spirit was slowly and steadily being crushed. Emma is a fighter and she fights for those she loves. She was the only one who my sister could not push away or bully. She stuck steadfast in her love for Catherine, coming every summer in spite of all the curtailments. How could she see Catherine suffer every single day and not do anything about it?"

"Her alibi?" Nutters interrupted.

"Pickering could have fallen asleep. The Earl and Emma may have been aware of being followed and worked together to kill my sister once the coast was clear."

The Duke fell silent. The others stirred as if awakening from a trance. They waited a few moments for the Duke to continue and when he did not, they moved to pour themselves tea or wine.

Soft murmurs soon became louder as they all discussed the Duke's observations. The clock chimed ten and they wondered if no more was to come.

Pickering entered the room with a tray of refreshments, dispelling the thought that the session was now over. They were in for a long night.

No one had any desire to eat, and the Duke finally gestured to Pickering to remain, "It is not pleasant talking about people I love in such a ruthless manner. I am being as impartial as I can. It would not be fair if I only dissected the strangers or friends present and spared my own family. It pains me as much as it is hurting all of you. Mr Barker, would you like a cigar?"

Mr Barker jumped at the sudden change of subject and shook his head.

The Duke passed the box to Lord Raikes, and then continued. "Allow me to speak of your daughter, Mr Barker,"

Mr Barker nodded worriedly.

"Prudence was being blackmailed by my sister, and we all know that, since the evidence was found in the form of letters and the brooch. I will not go into details of what she was being blackmailed for. I hope anyone who is aware of the reasons will keep it to themselves. She has a strong motive and no one to vouch for her innocence. Now, I beg your indulgence a little further by discussing your wife."

Mrs Barker fidgeted under all the eyes that suddenly turned towards her. She absently picked up a bowl on the table near her and dug the spoon into an elderberry ice. She did not lift the spoon to her mouth as she waited for the Duke to continue.

"She too was being blackmailed. She gave me her reasons, and unfortunately it was not the complete truth. After discovering the murder, I instructed Pickering and a man provided by Nutters to stand guard outside my sister's door. It was lucky I thought of it in spite of my state of shock. Mrs Barker and Mr Barker were seen lurking around outside the door. They had no reason to venture into that part of the house as their room falls in the opposite direction. They have visited my home often enough to know their way around, so their excuse of getting lost did not sit well with me. I, therefore, searched through every piece of paper in my sister's room and found the reason. Mr Barker was involved in the embezzlement of a large sum of money. That was the true reason for the blackmail. I suspected Mrs Barker was lying the moment she told me she was afraid her husband would find out about her extramarital affairs. Her husband, as we all know, could not have been unaware of his wife's indiscretions, as she has no qualms flirting outrageously in front of him. I think he even encourages it to further his own means."

Mr Barker, for once, remained silent. Mrs Barker had dropped a spoonful of ice on her lap, where it now sat melting into her skirts.

The Duke tapped an unlit cigar on the table. "I then conducted an experiment. I asked Nutters to go into Mrs Barker's room when she was not present. I similarly entered Mr Barker's room and closed the connecting door. The servants had already assured me that the door between their rooms has remained closed for years. They often know such things, and it would be too much of a coincidence if the door were suddenly opened on the night of the murder. I then asked Nutters to open the main door and slip out into the hallway. According to Mr Barker, he had heard his wife leave in the middle of the night. Imagine my surprise when I found that I could not hear a thing. I then requested a younger servant to take my place to ensure nothing was wrong with my hearing. He, too, could not tell when Nutters departed the room. I concluded that the two had planned to face my sister together. I am also sure they had an ugly argument with her. The reason was the brooch. My sister had failed to locate the basket left by Prudence. She expected the girl would come and see her that night with a valid excuse. She did not think Prudence would dare to ignore her instructions without an explanation. Accordingly, she had pulled out the brooch to gloat and kept it next to her as a reminder to Prudence as to who held the reins. She was a cruel woman. Instead, Mr Barker and Mrs Barker arrived in her room to reason with her. They noticed the brooch lying on the bed and realised who else she had been blackmailing; hence, they argued and perhaps in a heated moment . . . killed her."

"We did not kill her," Mrs Barker whispered, "It is true, we fought bitterly, for I could not stand the thought of my daughter being subjected to the same misery as I was. It was heartless to use such a young girl for her means. It was the first time that I knew of it, and I could no longer control my emotions. I was so angry . . . I could have killed her, but I did not!"

The Duke just glanced at her blandly and continued as if he had never been interrupted, "I had briefly touched upon the topic of Lady Babbage's son yesterday. I want to expand on that and tell you some more about him. I had mentioned that each one of you has seen him but not met him. His name is Joseph Babbage, and he has been working as an under-gardener on the estate. I was not aware of this until a few days ago when one of my men overheard him speaking to my sister. He was planning to rob the house on the night of the murder. That is why I had requested Pickering to bar the entrance to the servant quarters and stay within the main house."

"So did he kill her?" the Earl asked.

The Duke did not immediately answer. Then he spoke slowly, "I was told that a blonde man with a knife was seen in the corridor. I had assumed our killer was Joe. It would have been a convenient solution that protected every member of my family, and I would have gotten rid of the rogue. Unfortunately, he became aware of the fact that I knew of his planned robbery. Lady Babbage may have overheard my conversation with Pickering and warned him. I do not know for sure. He left right after dinner and went to the local pub in the village. He drank himself into a stupor and passed out on the table. The pub owner threw him out on the street, where he lay until the morning. I did not believe his story until the villagers confirmed it."

"Then who is the blonde man?" the Earl wondered aloud.

"There is only one man in this house who is tall and blonde, and that happens to be . . . you, Lord Richard Hamilton."

Chapter 30

The Earl turned white, and Emma emitted a strangled sound.

"Let me continue. I know you did not commit the crime, since Pickering followed you around the whole night in the mistaken belief that you had been convinced by Lady Babbage to rob me. He never liked the look of you, which as it turns out is lucky for you, since you have a watertight alibi from two people I trust. Yes, I trust you, Emma, because I know you," the Duke said, looking at her, "I also believe you because your actions that night do not make sense otherwise. Why would the two of you hunt for proof that Lady Babbage was a blackmailer if you intended to kill her? What was the point if, by the end of it, she would be dead and Prudence safe? You had no idea Pickering was following you or that I had asked him to stay that night. Even if you had somehow found out, this whole act of hunting for the note just to ward off suspicion did not make sense. What could you gain by it? The murder would not have been made any easier."

He turned to address Mr and Mrs Barker, "You also had a reason to commit murder, and you were the last to see her alive. I again question your actions on that night. If you had murdered my sister, then the last thing you would want is to be seen returning from the direction of the victim's room. The murder was planned, please remember, since the weapon used was a butcher knife which is not an object ordinarily found lying around in one's rooms. It was not an act of momentary passion. If it were planned, then why, Mr Barker, would you allow yourself to be foolishly seen? You did not even attempt to conceal your identity. Now I come to the biggest question. If you or Prudence murdered her, then why in the world would you leave the letters and brooch in her room after the act? The letter referring to the embezzlement was still there, as well as the letters for

Prudence. If you had left it as a clever ploy to ward of suspicion, then why did you try and return to her room later that day? If you knew the woman was dead, you could have fetched it all through the hours before the body was discovered. Mrs Barker is well aware of my character. She knows I will not let any financial misconduct go unpunished. In the same manner, why would Prudence kill her to conceal her secret and then leave the letters airing those very secrets out for all to read?"

He paused to take a deep breath. His eyes softened as he looked towards his daughter. He patted the arm of his chair, hoping she would come and sit by him.

She ignored him, her face expressionless.

The Duke sighed and swallowed some whisky to wet his dry throat. His voice lost its deep, musical tone, instead becoming ragged and rough as he continued to speak. "Catherine and Lord Raikes, why did I discount them? Let me start with Lord Raikes. I spent considerable time learning his character. I knew my daughter was growing attached to him, and Lord Raikes never tried to hide his feelings. I know he is an intelligent man and well-travelled. I also know he studied medicine along with Lord Hamilton. If a man like that had to commit murder, what would he do? He would use his experience and knowledge. He would do the job so neatly that no one would be able to tell that the death had not been natural. He understands medicine and he understands poison. He could have used some rare roots to bring about heart failure or leaves to cause a death coma. Why would he not slip some deathly herb into her cup instead of stabbing her with a knife? The knife made it obvious that it was murder and that meant Catherine could be implicated. He loves Catherine, and the last thing he would want is to have suspicion fall on her."

He turned once more to face his daughter, "You must be wondering by now why I first give a long speech implicating everyone and then spend the next hour proving how they are innocent. I am not doing this because it gives me any perverse satisfaction. The reason is that I want the murderer to know why everyone else is eliminated and how no other suspect is left. I do not want the person to have any room to escape what is coming. The murderer is well aware of all the motives each one of you had. Your actions prove your innocence, trapping the murderer. So I beg you to indulge my monologues a little longer."

The people in the room became tense, realising that not many of them were left to be analysed. It was becoming increasingly obvious that the Duke knew who had killed his sister and he was patiently and methodically eliminating each one of them, moving closer to the culprit.

"I know that if I beseech you to believe me, on the basis of a father's insight, that his daughter did not commit such a heinous act, then no one would believe me. Therefore, I must strive to convince you with practical deduction. If Catherine had killed her aunt, then she could hardly expect her own father to call her out for it. She would have felt safe committing the crime making her the most dangerous and obvious suspect."

Lord Raikes gripped Catherine's hand, his eyes like two deep, dark wells of fury. She gave him a strained smile and nodded for her father to continue.

The Duke looked away from the entwined hands choosing to pin his gaze on the blazing fire instead. "We know that the murder was committed after Mrs Barker left my sister's room just after one in the morning. Around that time Catherine visited Lord Raikes in his room and he followed her back to her room. Prudence was witness to the fact."

Prudence nervously murmured an agreement.

The Duke looked up, his emotions no longer in control. He spoke quickly and agitatedly, "Imagine for a moment that she had planned the entire thing. At one o'clock, she sat ready and waiting aware that in the morning I would investigate my sister's death. In such circumstances, would she go to a strange man's room, a man she believed was her beloved cousin's betrothed before venturing off to kill my sister? Would she do so knowing that questions would be asked and Lord Raikes would have to confess his night's activities? Prudence saw her as well, and even if Raikes decided to keep silent, she might not. And since Lord Raikes went to Catherine's room, which is closest to her Aunt's, he would have been the other person implicated. Her growing regard for him is obvious. A murderer would have ensured that he or she stayed out of sight, and, yet, she knew at least two people saw her out of bed at the time of the murder."

He then called Pickering to his side.

"You are all wondering why I have not suspected Pickering? Why have I left him off the suspect list from the very beginning? What has he done to deserve my trust? Again I must convince you through deduction rather than sentiment. Lady Babbage refused to acknowledge anyone not of her class. The amount of money her son required was large. A mere butler could not provide such sums on the salary he makes. He has been my eyes and ears for a long time. He was the first person to discover my sister's dark activities. He did not wait for proof, but immediately informed me of what he had discovered. He knows me well enough to not dither on such important matters. I knew he had no reason to lie to me. Now, what could he gain from murdering my sister? Did he hold a secret infatuation for her and was denied her favours? Or perhaps she had slighted him on more than one occasion. He works in the kitchen and could easily procure a knife. He knew of the blackmail being conducted and how many people had a reason to kill her. It would be difficult to pin it on one single person. He could have also been aware of all those people who were out of bed that night, giving him the perfect opportunity. He knew of at least two people, Emma and the Earl. He had even noticed Mr and Mrs Barker awake on the night of the murder. He had my permission to roam the house that night. What could be a more ideal situation?"

Mr Barker and the Earl leaned forward in their seats. Pickering stuffed all his fingers in his mouth to muffle the sound of his chattering teeth.

The Duke sent the butler a reassuring look. "He did not kill her for those very same reasons. He knew I was aware he was within the household that night. A servant would never believe he would be trusted over other members of the household. Unfortunately, they are the first to be suspected. If you remember, upon hearing of my sister's murder, Mr Barker immediately said that a servant did it. The last thing Pickering would have used to commit the crime was the butcher's knife, for it came directly from the kitchens, and hence pointed straight at him. The moment my eyes fell on the blade, I knew he was innocent."

"But then what about the blonde man seen roaming that night with a blade. Who was he?" Nutters asked, caught in the web the Duke had been weaving.

"Precisely! That is why I must now come to its source."

Everyone turned to stare at the last person left to be discussed.

"There was only one person who always had a reason to roam at night, only one person whose presence in the hallways at one in the morning would be overlooked as a common occurrence. The insinuation that a blonde man with a blade committed the crime came from the mouth of my dear wife, the Duchess. She had been aware of my sister's dark habit of blackmailing people. She knew who was being blackmailed and how many people had reason to do away with her. She was the only one who had no reason to remove the incriminating blackmail letters. She was also aware of Joe's existence. That is why the entire drama of seeing a vision or a ghost of a tall blonde man with a blade was played out for my benefit. What she did not know was that I had the doors locked that day or that Pickering was keeping so close an eye on things. The fates played a cruel joke on her. Everyone was out of bed that night, in a sense aiding her plans, though their actions that night proved their innocence. Even Joe had been lucky enough to get inebriated — "

"Oh, I have had enough," the Duchess said irritably. She leapt up, pulling Prudence along with her. A glint of metal sparkled in her hand in the firelight.

The Duke was the first to realise that she held a tiny pistol jabbed into Prudence's side.

Someone let out a horrified shriek. The shout didn't even procure a blink from the Duke who kept his eyes trained on his wife.

"I will say what I need to and then leave you all in peace. I suppose you know?" the Duchess asked, lifting her brow at the Duke.

He nodded.

"Fine, let me enlighten the rest. You have been speaking long enough these last two days. I am getting heartily sick of your voice. Now, credit me with the same respect you all afforded the Duke and stay silent while I speak," she said, glaring around the room.

No one moved an inch. Satisfied, she continued. "I was a famous burglar in Italy, and I have conducted some fabulous thefts in my days."

Catherine gasped in shock.

The Duchess sent her step daughter a fond look and continued, "I fled from there when my identity was discovered. I found the Duke ripe for plucking, still grieving for his dead wife. I was going to steal his precious heirlooms, but by then I was tired of running. I fashioned myself into something exotic, different from prim English misses. He fell in love with me. Imagine my surprise when he actually proposed. I would have been content as his mistress."

"I married you because I respected you and believed you deserved more than a common mistress," the Duke said softly.

The Duchess rolled her eyes, "How dull you are, even at such an exciting moment! If you had been livelier, perhaps I wouldn't have become so bored after marriage. My life had been filled with excitement, romance, and drama in Italy, while here I was nothing but a boring old Duchess with dozens of rules to follow. I felt like a caged pigeon whose wings had been clipped. It was difficult," she said her eyes on Emma. "Surely you can understand that?"

Emma couldn't, but she schooled her horrified expression and said, "I understand. You couldn't flutter."

"Precisely," the Duchess cried. "I couldn't flutter. I could no longer fly. I became restless and soon got in touch with my old accomplices. I could only advise them as to techniques and plots through letters, yet, those moments gave me a thrill like in the olden days. Then my dearly departed sister-in-law discovered my secret. She tried to blackmail me, threatening to tell the Duke."

"Why didn't you go back to where you came from?" Catherine dared to ask. "Left my poor father in peace."

The Duchess narrowed her eyes and pressed the pistol into Prudence's spine making her squeak. "However much I wanted to return to my old life, I could not afford to do that. I had created such a comfortable place here with all its luxuries. Besides, I am older and no more as nimble. I can no longer scale walls or run as fast. My feigned madness allowed me to write late into the night to my friends. I loved vexing everyone with my little speeches of the spirit world. No one took me seriously, and that suited me fine. That is exactly what I wanted. Perhaps I planned to run away for a short time and cheat some rich man of his treasures for the fun of it. I could then return to my home at my convenience, and what could one say to a mad woman? It was all so perfect until . . . she spoiled it all. I placated her with some paltry sums, but her demands kept increasing. I could take it no more. I knew she was blackmailing some of you, and I knew of this whole game of the Earl and Joe being present. It was the perfect opportunity, so I stole into her room while she slept and stabbed her."

"Are you sorry?" Emma asked.

"I did the Duke a favour," the Duchess said. An odd emotion flickered momentarily on her face. "With her gone every single person in this room has benefitted. Am I sorry? No. I am glad I did it and if I had to, I would do so again and again and again."

"Put the pistol down," the Duke said carefully. "We can talk about this."

She kept her eye on the Duke as she brutally twisted the cold muzzle into Prudence's back forcing her to stand. She began inching her way towards the door. "No more talking. I know you and your noble, humdrum heart. You will not spare me no matter what sweet words you might utter now. I was smart enough to plan my escape if I were discovered. I, for one, have never underestimated your intelligence," she said, grinning with a mad light dancing in her eyes. "Now, my friends wait in the dark night, so I bid you adieu."

She dragged Prudence out the front door and into the garden, and no one dared stop her.

A carriage sat waiting on the outskirts. She climbed into it, pushing Prudence to the ground. She kept the pistol trained on the girl until the carriage went out of sight.

"Will you follow her, Your Grace?" Pickering asked.

"We will never catch her. She would have planned it well," the Duke replied sadly.

"Did you know?" Catherine asked her father.

"I became suspicious after my sister hinted that I should look into my wife's past. I started keeping a closer eye on the Duchess and noticed how astute she was. I wondered if she was pretending to be mad and could not understand her reasons for doing so. I hired Nutters to investigate. I had started the investigation out of curiosity, wondering where she came from, what kind of madness she had, and whether it ran in the family, since I was expected to produce an heir. It took me a long time to find out the truth . . . My sister tried to tell me a few days before she died . . . I think my wife had refused to play her games anymore. I had brushed my sister aside and warned her to stay out of my business. I did not want to confess that I suspected the same thing. I wanted the proof that Nutters was going to procure for me before I took any action. I became worried having her under the same roof, and I think somewhere deep in my heart, I knew what she was capable of . . . and she proved me right."

Catherine slipped her hand through his and led him inside. He looked as if he had aged years in those last few moments.

It was a considerable time before the house was calm again.

Epilogue

"Lord Raikes," Catherine said, crushing her white silk gown with her fingers.

"Call me, William."

"Don't you think our wedding has happened too soon? You did promise me a courtship. Perhaps we should wait a while before . . . " Catherine said nervously.

"Before?" he prompted, smiling.

"Well, you know?"

"No, I don't. Elaborate, my dear. The wedding wine is making me feel a bit dim," he said wickedly.

"To become husband and wife . . . "

"Too late. We are already married."

"I mean to . . . to . . . share the bed," she whispered finally.

Lord William Raikes stared at his trembling wife, his face serious.

"Answer me first. Do you love me?"

Catherine bit her lip and then slowly lifted her lashes. She saw his intense expression and understood his fear. She knew he loved her, and he was afraid that once more he would be rejected by his love.

Her heart squeezed painfully and she caught his hand in hers and nodded, her eyes darkening with emotion.

He grinned in delight, "Then I no longer have to woo you. As for not sharing the bed, then you are in for a disappointment."

Then they did, and she was not disappointed.

❖ ❖ ❖

Emma sat in her wedding finery in her new home. She watched the Earl pour them a glass of wine.

"So you admit the Duke is far cleverer than you?" Emma asked, pulling the pins out of her hair.

"I do not! The point of the wager was to show that the Duke could be fooled, and he was fooled by his wife no less . . . for ten whole years!" the Earl replied.

"Humph, but you lost. You did not prove it. He knew who you were from the very beginning."

"Yes, but the point is that he was duped, and I managed the end I wanted."

"What's that?"

"Why, marrying you within two months. I even got my poor friend married off to your cousin in the bargain."

"That was not your doing. You could not have imagined that they would fall in love."

The Earl grinned as he leaned in for a kiss, "Are you sure about that, my love?"

Emma eyed her husband sceptically. He pushed her back on the bed and dived under the covers. He had the rest of his life to convince her of his intelligence. For the moment, he had work to do . . .

"Ooh, is this even possible?"

"Yes, and more."

"Oh, I don't think . . . I see . . . "

"There is more . . . "

"Nooo"

"Yes"

"Ah, I see now what you mean."

"You will see a lot more, my dear, I am just getting started."

And they lived happily ever after.

❖ ❖ ❖

The Duchess of Arden tapped the ash off her cigar, "So, he is the richest man in all of France?" she asked huskily, sizing up her prey.

"He is a sharp one. He didn't make all that money by acting a fool."

Her full lips curved into half a smile.

"If I could dupe the Duke, then this frog-faced man is hardly competition."

"Don't be over confident, he is brilliant. Be careful, I think you have met your match."

"I hope so," she whispered, throwing the glowing stub away.

She took a sip of her whisky and arranged her face into a helpless expression before sashaying towards her new target.

The End

ABOUT THE AUTHOR

Anya Wylde lives in Ireland along with her husband and a fat French poodle (now on a diet). She can cook a mean curry, and her idea of exercise is occasionally stretching her toes. She holds a degree in English literature and adores reading and writing. Connect with Anya Wylde on Facebook, Twitter, Pinterest, or Google+ to be notified about her upcoming releases, or follow her on her Amazon Author Page.

Website: www.anyawylde.com

Other Books By The Author

Regency Romantic comedy
Penelope
Seeking Philbert Woodbead
Regency Mystery
Murder At Rudhall Manor
Fantasy Novella
Ever After
Contemporary Romance
Love Muffin And Chai Latte